EXTRATERRESTRIAL CREDIT

A COLLECTION OF THE PS238 COMIC BOOK, VOLUME V
ISSUES #22 THROUGH #27

BY AARON WILLIAMS

PUBLISHED BY DO GOODER PRESS
www.dogooderpress.com

E-mail: aaron@ps238.com
Marketing & Advertising: sales@dogooderpress.com

Printed in Canada • First Printing, March 2008 • ISBN 1-933288-42-6

WHEN WE LAST LEFT OUR HEROES...

Cecil Holmes, a student suspicious of just about everyone he meets (and in some cases, rightly so), is on the lookout for aliens. As a member of the Bureau of Alien Management, he's been vigilantly watching his fellow students who seem to have something odd about them....

...which is only natural since a great many of them are superheroes and attend classes at ps238, located three miles below Cecil's school.

The students have already had many amazing adventures, even the defeating of a bully who could teleport!

And a few of them have run into mysterious men in golden armor who seem intent on capturing super-kids for an unknown purpose.

One of the student body isn't even from this planet. Prospero, who came to Earth speaking a strange language and seemingly predicting a great catastrophe has been watching the stars for evidence of offworld activity...

...and boy was there activity! An alien probe has landed on Earth and taken Captain Clarinet as its prisoner! Moon Shadow, the alter-ego of non-super-powered ps238 student Tyler Marlocke, tried to rescue the Captain and instead became snared in the alien machine's grasp as well!

WHAT HAPPENS NEXT?! READ ON AND FIND OUT!

Genius is a nuisance, and it is the duty of schools and colleges to abate it by setting genius traps in its way.

- Samuel Butler

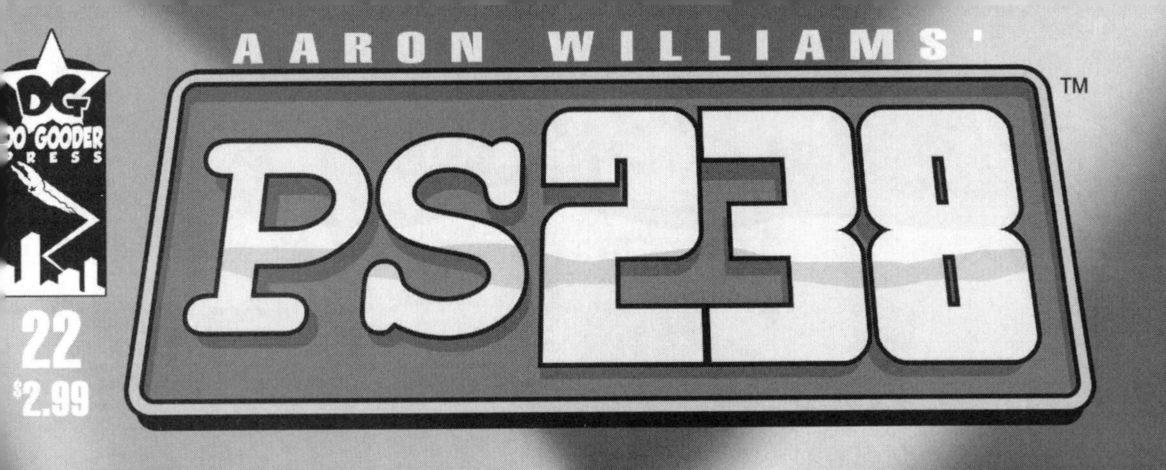

AGENT CECIL HOLMES
BUREAU OF ALIEN MONITORING
PLAYGROUND: 12:36 AM

B·A·M
BUREAU OF ALIEN MONITORING
AGENT FIRST CLASS

- HE IS OUR FIRST LINE OF DEFENSE.
- HE IS ABOUT TO MEET A HOSTILE EXTRATERRESTRIAL AT SCHOOL.
- HE WANTS YOU TO REMEMBER HIS SLUMBER PARTY IS NEXT MONTH.
- GODSPEED, AGENT HOLMES.

PS238
THE SCHOOL FOR METAPRODIGY CHILDREN
BY AARON WILLIAMS
WHY DID YOU COME AFTER ME?! IT CANT EVEN HURT ME!
LEAVE HIM ALONE!!!
IT SOUNDS LIKE A MACHINE!
A MACHINE.
LIKE DOCTOR IRONS WAS!
MAGNET!
CLICK

WONGA! WONGA! WONGA! WONGA!
I TURNED MY GRAPPLER MAGNET ON AS HIGH AS IT WOULD GO. I DON'T KNOW HOW LONG THAT'LL MESS UP THE--
LOOK! THE HATCH-THING IS OPEN! GET OUT! QUICK, BEFORE IT CLOSES UP AGAIN!
BUT I CAME TO GET YOU OUT OF HERE!
I DIDN'T ASK YOU TO! NOW LEAVE! IT CAN'T HURT ME! IT TRIED AND NOTHING--
YOU BROUGHT MY CLARINET! GIVE IT TO ME!
NOW WHAT?
NOW I'MA GOIN' TOOF FAVE YOUF!

BLAAT!
WHO ARE YOU, CHILD, AND WHAT DID YOU DO? THE ALIEN SEEMED TO WEAKEN FOR A MOMENT.
BUT IT LOOKS LIKE IT'S BACK ON IT'S FEET... OR WHATEVER...
CAPTAIN CLARINET IS STILL IN THERE!
I HOPE THAT HELMET WILL PROTECT MOON SHADOW'S EARS...
IT'S GETTING AWAY!
OKAY, EVERYONE GET CLEAR. I'M GOING TO GIVE MY "SEISMIC STOMP" A TRY.
BUT BEFORE COACH ROCKSLIDE CAN PUT HIS FOOT DOWN...

CAN WE NOT TELL MY MOM AND DAD ABOUT THIS?!
I CAN'T HEAR YOU IF YOU'RE SAYING ANYTHING! MY HEARING WILL COME BACK IN A FEW MINUTES, OKAY?!
MOON SHADOW RETURNS TO THE REVENANT'S PLANE...
I'M GLAD YOU FEEL THE SAME WAY I DO ABOUT OVERSTAYING YOUR WELCOME.
I WAS AFRAID THEY'D MAKE ME TALK TO RON SOME MORE. I DON'T KNOW WHAT TO SAY TO HIM. I MEAN...
HIS PARENTS SPLITTING UP ISN'T HIS FAULT, BUT HE THINKS IT IS, AND HE'S READY TO GIVE UP EITHER USING HIS POWERS OR PLAYING HIS MUSIC, AND BOTH IDEAS SOUND CRAZY!
HE'S LOOKING FOR CONTROL. HIS HOME HAS GONE TOPSY-TURVY, AND HE WANTS TO FIX IT BY DOING SOMETHING.
I DON'T THINK THAT'LL WORK.
I DON'T BELIEVE SO, EITHER.
MAYBE... COULD I WRITE HIM A LETTER OR SOMETHING?
OH, WE CAN DO BETTER THAN THAT. CAN YOU THINK OF AN APPROPRIATE MESSAGE IN ABOUT TEN MINUTES?

ABOUT AN HOUR LATER, AT RON'S HOUSE...
ARE YOU SURE YOU'RE ALL RIGHT? EVEN THOUGH IT DIDN'T HURT, IT COULD STILL HAVE BEEN A PRETTY SCARY--
I'M FINE, MOM.
OKAY. DON'T FORGET THAT WE'RE SUPPOSED TO TALK WITH MISTER BAIN TOMORROW ABOUT... THAT TELEPORTING BOY.
IS DAD HOME TONIGHT?
WE TALKED ABOUT THIS, RON. HE'LL VISIT TOMORROW FOR OUR MEETING WITH MISTER BAIN. THEN HE'LL BE STAYING IN NEW YORK WHILE--
I WANT TO SLEEP NOW ANYWAY. G'NIGHT.
DEET-DEET-DEET-DEET-DEET-DEET-DEET-DEET-DEET
click!
BEGINNING PLAYBACK. STAND BY...

CAPTAIN CLARINET? IT'S MOON SHADOW. YOU ASKED ME IF I THOUGHT YOU SHOULD STOP BEING A KID WHO LOVES HIS MUSIC OR STOP BEING A KID WHO'S GOING TO BE A SUPERHERO SOMEDAY.
I DON'T THINK YOU CAN GIVE UP YOUR MUSIC, BECAUSE IF IT WASN'T IMPORTANT TO YOU, YOU WOULDN'T HAVE NAMED YOURSELF AFTER IT. AND IF BEING HELPFUL WITH YOUR POWERS WASN'T IMPORTANT, TOO, YOU WOULDN'T HAVE PICKED A HERO NAME AT ALL.
YOU SAID CHOOSING WOULD MAKE EITHER YOUR MOM OR YOUR DAD HAPPY, BUT I DON'T THINK THAT'S TRUE. I KNOW I CAN'T MAKE MY PARENTS HAPPY, SO YOU PROBABLY CAN'T FIX WHATEVER IS WRONG WITH YOURS.
I DON'T KNOW WHAT IT'S LIKE TO HAVE YOUR MOM AND DAD NOT BE TOGETHER. I'LL BET IT HURTS A WHOLE LOT. BUT YOU HAVE FRIENDS, RON. AND YOU'RE A GOOD PERSON. DON'T LOSE THAT.
OH, THANKS FOR SAVING ME FROM THAT... WHATEVER IT WAS. I REALLY, REALLY, APPRECIATE IT.
END MESSAGE.
SLAM!!

THE FOLLOWING MORNING, BEFORE CLASS...
GOOD MORNING, EVERYONE. HERSCHEL, DO YOU EVER SLEEP?
EVERY MONTH OR SO. WORKIN' WITH AN ANDROID WILL MAKE YOU SELF-CONSCIOUS ABOUT YOUR WORK ETHIC.
WE'RE STILL ANALYZING THE REMAINS, AND IT'S NOT THE FACT THAT IT'S A... WHAT DID YOU CALL IT, HERSCHEL? A "CYBER-SQUID ON STEROIDS." THAT'S NOT WHAT'S WORRISOME.
WHAT IS? OTHER THAN THAT IT'S COMPLETELY DISGUSTING...
THE SIGNAL PULSE IT SENT RIGHT BEFORE IT EXPLODED.
SIGNAL PULSE?
YEAH. WE DIDN'T GET ALL OF IT, AND WE'RE HAVIN' A DEVIL OF A TIME DECIPHERING IT, BUT MOST OF IT SEEMS TO BE DNA SEQUENCES.
WHOEVER SENT IT KNOWS THERE'S LIFE ON THIS PLANET, AND THEY MIGHT HAVE THE HUMAN GENOME. IT'S POSSIBLE THE DATA CAME FROM THE BOY IN THE FOOTBALL HELMET.
WE THINK THAT WAS MOON SHADOW.
WHO?
DIDN'T YOU READ THE REPORT THAT AMERICAN EAGLE GAVE CRANSTON ABOUT FIGHTIN' CHARLES?
I ADMIT I'VE BEEN A BIT PREOCCUPIED LATELY.
YOU OUGHTA READ IT, OR DOWNLOAD IT, OR WHATEVER. SHE WRITES LIKE A LITTLE TOM CLANCY, BUT SHE MAKES THIS MOON SHADOW SOUND LIKE A LITTLE MILITARY GENIUS.
OH. I SEE.
YES, SHE DOES WRITE A BIT LIKE-- WAIT A MINUTE...
POSITRON ONE UPLINK RE: POSITRON TWO. INCOMING DATA STREAM RELEVANT TO CURRENT INQUIRIES. PLEASE PROCESS AND PROCEED.

MOMENTS EARLIER, AT THE K-SQUARE CONVENIENCE STORE...
SHOULDN'T YOU BE IN SCHOOL?
I'LL GET GOING SOON. SINCE I STARTED THIS NEW JOB, THOUGH, I CAN'T FUNCTION WITHOUT MY MORNING CUP OF MOUNTAIN DEW WITH A SHOT OF CHERRY, YOU KNOW?
CURSE OF THE WORKING MAN, I GUESS.
OH-KAY...
WHERE'S DIANA? SHE USUALLY WORKS THE MORNING SHIFT.
OH, UM... SHE WENT ON VACATION.
WHEN WILL SHE BE BACK?
I WISH I KNEW.
SO WHAT'S WITH THE GOGGLES?
HUH? OH. I FORGOT I HAD THOSE ON.
AND I NOTICED THE LAB COAT HUNG ON THE PEG IN THE OFFICE. IS THAT YOURS?
YOU NOTICE A LOT OF THINGS, DON'T YOU?
"VIGILANCE."
MORE THAN YOU KNOW. THE PRICE OF LIBERTY IS ETERNAL VILLAGES.
RIGHT.
LOOK, KID, I'VE GOT TO MOP UP AND--
INCOMING NETWORK MESSAGE RE: MISSING PERSONS, NODE P-5, SUBJUNCTION GAMMA. PROCEED BASED ON INFORMATION TO FOLLOW...0010101011010101010101010000101
0101001010101010101001010101010101010110111
10101010010101010101001001001101011110010
10100101010101010100101010010111010100100
1001001111010101010
101010101010000
1101011011010
0101010101010
LOOK, KID, I'VE GOT TO LOCK UP FOR A WHILE. YOU NEED TO GO.

IT'S NOT EVEN SEVEN-THIRTY YET.
AND YOU'VE GOT TO GET TO SCHOOL.
COME BACK AFTER CLASSES AND I'LL LET YOU MIX EVERY CAFFEINATED DRINK I'VE GOT.
CONVEN
CONVEN
CONVEN
MINUTES LATER...
SAM'S SWAP SHOP
YARK!
YOU SURE THIS IS THE PLACE?
01001010100101110101001
00100100111101010101001
010010100101010010101010
OKAY. FINE, I'LL KEEP THE LINK OPEN, BUT NO RIFFLING THROUGH MY FILES. I DON'T NEED ANOTHER CRITIQUE OF MY MP3 COLLECTION.
KRACK!

THANK GOD YOU CAME! I THOUGHT WE'D NEVER GET OUTTA THERE!
HE LEFT US! AN' THEN THAT GREEN KID MADE A HOLE IN THE ROOF, BUT WE COULDN'T CLIMB OUT!
AN' IT WAS COLD AT NIGHT! AND WE YELLED AND YELLED AND--
TRAGIC STORY. BUT YOU AREN'T OUT OF THE WOODS YET. CHARLES MADE SOMEONE DISAPPEAR: THE LADY THAT WORKED AT K-SQUARE.
UH... YEAH. HE TOLD US ABOUT THAT.
THAT'S WHERE HE GOT ALL THE STUFF WE'VE BEEN EATIN' WHILE WE WERE LOCKED IN HERE.
WHERE DID HE TAKE HER?
NOWHERE.
YEAH. NOWHERE.
BOYS TRESPASSING IN A BUILDING FILLED WITH STOLEN CANDY BARS DON'T GET AMNESIA IF THEY'RE SMART. SHE'S NOT "NOWHERE." WHERE'D CHARLES TAKE HER?
HE CALLED IT "NOWHERE." IT'S... SOMEWHERE HE COULD TELEPORT HIMSELF TO.
RIGHT BEFORE HE FOUGHT WITH THESE KIDS IN CAPES, HE SAID I COULD HAVE THE K-SQUARE.
I ASKED HIM "WHAT ABOUT THAT LADY WHO KICKS US OUT?" AND HE SAID "I TOOK HER TO NOWHERE TODAY. SHE'S GONE FOREVER, ON THIS ROCK FLOATING IN OUTER SPACE."
A ROCK IN SPACE?
THAT'S WHAT WE SAID, AND CHARLES SAID IT WAS SOMEWHERE HE FOUND BY ACCIDENT, AND HE WAS GONNA USE IT FOR PEOPLE HE DIDN'T LIKE, BUT WE AIN'T SEEN HIM FOR DAYS!

YOU'RE SURE THAT'S ALL HE SAID?
I SWEAR!
YEAH, HE'LL TELL YOU!
WHY DON'T YOU ASK CHARLES?
HE'S GONE. NOBODY'S SEEN HIM IN DAYS.
MAYBE HE WENT TO NOWHERE, TOO.
MAYBE HE'S MAD AT US. MAYBE THAT'S WHY HE LEFT US HERE.
OR THOSE KIDS GOT HIM!
IF HE'S MAD AT US...
CAN WE, LIKE, GO NOW, MISTER?
WE WON'T MESS WITH ANOTHER K-SQUARE AGAIN, WE SWEAR!
WE THINK WE MIGHT WANNA MOVE TO ANOTHER STATE.
KNOCK YOURSELVES OUT.
DID THAT MAKE ANY SENSE TO YOU?
01001010010101010010101010
01001010100101110101001
0010010011110101010101001
ME, NEITHER. YOU WANNA TRY SCANNING THE K-SQUARE WITH TACHYONS, AGAIN? I THOUGHT THAT ALMOST SHOWED US SOMETHING...
...BUT IF SHE'S GONE... LIKE, GONE-GONE... I HOPE SHE'S NOT CONSCIOUS ANYMORE. I DON'T THINK I COULD STAND BEING AWAY FROM MY FAMILY FOR SO LONG...
KID SPY™ SONIC EAR™
KID SPY™ SONIC EAR™

MINUTES LATER, AT A NEARBY DRIVE-THROUGH...
...AND EXTRA HASH BROWNS.
WOULD YOU LIKE TO TRY OUR FRENCH TOASTIES WITH MAPLE SYRUP?
NO! NO MORE SUGAR!
THAT WILL BE TEN-FIFTY. PLEASE COME TO THE WINDOW.
SUPERSONIC
HERO-SIZE BURGERS & FRIES!
YOU GOT THAT MUCH, GORDY?
YEAH. I FOUND CHARLES' MONEY JAR, REMEMBER?
I DON'T THINK I COULD HAVE EATEN ANY MORE TWINKIES OR CHOCOLATE BARS.
ME, NEITHER. I WISH HE HAD LIFTED SOME BURRITOS OR CORN FLAKES OR ANYTHING WITHOUT SUGAR IN IT!
D'YOU THINK HE'LL COME BACK?
I DUNNO. IF HE ASKS, THAT KID WITH THE GREEN COSTUME TOOK HIS MONEY, GOT IT?
RIGHT.
GOOD STORY. I'M SURE CHARLES IS DUMB ENOUGH TO BELIEVE IT.
OF COURSE, HE'D PROBABLY POUND YOU BOTH INTO A PULP ANYWAY FOR NOT PROTECTING HIS CASH.

ALIENS DON'T SHOW MUCH MERCY TO THIEVES.
WHA--? YOU'RE THAT CECIL NERD! YOU TELL ON US AND I'LL MAKE SURE YOU'RE IN A WORLD OF PAIN BEFORE HE GETS TO US!
YEAH!
WAIT. ALIENS?
LOOK, ALL I WANT IS MORE DETAILS ABOUT THAT "NOWHERE" PLACE. I'M SURE YOU DIDN'T THINK OF EVERYTHING WHEN YOU WERE WETTING YOUR PANTS BACK AT THE SWAP SHOP.
WHY SHOULD WE TELL YOU ANYTHING?
BECAUSE OF WHAT I HAVE IN MY COAT.
UNLESS YOU'VE GOT THE FRIGGIN' DEATH STAR IN THERE, WE AIN'T TELLING YOU SQUAT!
EXIT
FZZARK!
EXIT
THANK YOU, CITIZENS!
SUPERSONIC
TRY OUR HERO-SIZE TRIPLE WITH CHEESE COMBO!

AND THAT'S THE ONLY OTHER THING HE SAID! HONEST!
WE'VE GOTTA LEAVE TOWN, MAN! THIS PLACE IS CRAZY!
EXIT
SUPERSONIC
TRY OUR HERO SIZE TRIPLE
SO IT WAS A ROCK IN SPACE... WITH A FOUR-SQUARE DIAMOND ON IT? WHY DOES THAT SOUND--?
DEEDLE-DEET! DEEDLE-DEET! DEEDLE-DEET! DEEDLE-D
HELLO? YES, SIR, I DID FIRE MY WEAPON.
NO, SIR, NO CIVILIANS WERE HARMED, JUST A STATUE OF A SUPER-CLOWN. YES, SIR. AT SUPER-SONIC.
NO, SIR. IT WAS A DEMONSTRATION TO GET INFORMATION FROM TWO SUSPECTS. YES, SIR, FULLY JUSTIFIABLE. SHOULD I REVERSE IT?
NO? REALLY? I DIDN'T KNOW THAT ABOUT FAST FOOD. LIKE SOYLENT GREEN? WOW.
I'LL FILE A FULL REPORT BY THIS EVENING. THANK YOU SIR. YES, SIR, I SHOULD MAKE IT TO SCHOOL BEFORE HOMEROOM.
YOU, TOO, SIR. GOOD-BYE.
I LIKE THIS NEW BUREAU DIRECTOR; WITH HIM IN CHARGE, WE COULD WIN AGAINST THE ALIENS, I JUST KNOW IT!
I THINK I KNOW WHO CAN TELL ME MORE ABOUT "NOWHERE." I HOPE HE COMES TO SCHOOL TODAY...

LATER THAT MORNING IN PS238, JUST BEFORE LUNCH...
YAWWWNNN!
TYLER? I WISH TO TALK WITH YOU.
INTERNSHIPS
MORE...
HUH? OH. SURE, MALPHAST. WHAT'S UP?
CLASSES
AFTER SCHOOL
YOU SEEM UNRESTED.
I WAS UP LATE LAST NIGHT.
I SEE. I DON'T SLEEP AS YOU DO, BUT I THINK MURPHY GAVE ME ENOUGH INFORMATION ABOUT IT TO HELP.
HOLD STILL...
WHOA! I FEEL... GOOD! WHAT DID YOU DO?
I CAN'T EXPLAIN IT IN WORDS YOU'D UNDERSTAND. REST ASSURED YOUR SOUL WILL RECOVER IN TIME.
MY WHAT?
CECIL WANTED ME TO GIVE YOU A MESSAGE. HE SAID HE HAS A LEAD ON THE MISSING K-SQUARE MANAGER, BUT HE NEEDED MY HELP. AS HIS SUPERIOR OFFICER, HE WANTED YOUR PERMISSION FOR ME TO ASSIST HIM.
WILL YOU GIVE YOUR CONSENT?
UM... YES?
HE WILL BE PLEASED. AS AM I. I THINK I ENJOY PLAYING WITH YOU MORTALS!
GOOD DAY, FRIEND TYLER.
WHEN HE SAYS "PLAYING WITH MORTALS," I WONDER IF HE MEANS--
HE'S COMING! HE'S COMING HERE!
HUMPH!

EXCUSE ME, I DIDN'T SEE--
OH... OH, JEEZE.
ARE YOU OKAY, TYLER? I DIDN'T SEE YOU AND... OH, MAN. ARE YOU HURT?
WHRERGGGHGHHEEEE...
WOW. I REALLY KNOCKED THE WIND OUT OF YOUR SAILS. ARE YOU GOING TO BE OKAY?
OH, GOOD. I GUESS THAT'S WHY I WE SHOULDN'T RUN IN THE HALLS, ESPECIALLY IF WE'RE MADE OF METAL, HUH?
WELL, GUESS WHO'S COMING TO CAREER DAY IN A WEEK? GIVE UP?
WHRRZZZIIEEEE...
WIL WHEATON!
YOU KNOW, THE ACTOR? FROM STAR TREK? HE JUST CALLED TO CONFIRM! I CAN'T WAIT TO TELL PRINCIPAL CRANSTON! AND I'M GONNA ASK HIM TO SIGN MY STAR TREK DVDS!
WIL WHEATON, THAT IS, NOT PRINCIPAL CRANSTON.
WOW. I GOTTA STAY FOCUSED. HE'S A PROMINENT METAHUMAN CELEBRITY, HERE TO TELL THE STUDENTS ABOUT HIS CAREER PATH... BUT HE COULD STILL AUTOGRAPH SOME OF MY COLLECTION, RIGHT?
SSSSSURRRRRE...
IF YOU'RE GOING TO BE FINE, I'VE GOT TO TELL THE REST OF THE TEACHERS!
YOU GO ENJOY LUNCH ABOVEGROUND, AND IF YOU DON'T HAVE ANYTHING FOR MR. WHEATON TO SIGN, I CAN GIVE YOU ONE OF MY POSTERS. I'VE GOT LOTS OF DUPLICATES.
WHULP, I'LL SEE YOU LATER!

I CAN'T BELIEVE HE'S COMING! THIS IS GONNA BE SO COOL!
HEY, DOCTOR POSITRON! YOU LIKE STAR TREK, DON'T YOU?
SOON AFTER LUNCH...
...AND SO I'M KIND OF SORE BECAUSE... UM, I RAN INTO A BIG... METAL... DOOR, I GUESS.
THAT'S OKAY, BECAUSE I NEED TO BRING YOU UP TO DATE.
NOT THAT KICKBALL ISN'T FUN, BUT...
I SPENT THE MORNING RECESS COMPOSING MY REPORT TO THE BUREAU.
THE DIRECTOR CALLED ME TODAY, AND WE THINK WE MIGHT BE ON TO SOMETHING NEW IN THE CHARLES BRIGMAN CASE.
THE WHO CALLED ABOUT WHAT?
DON'T WORRY, I WON'T LET ANYTHING INCRIMINATING SLIP WHILE WE'RE IN PUBLIC. I JUST WANTED TO APPRISE YOU OF MY CASELOAD.
AND THANKS FOR LETTING ME PARTNER WITH MALPHAST. I THINK HE'S REALLY COMING TO LIKE EARTH, DON'T YOU?
UH--
BR-R-R-R-R-R-R-R-RING-G-G-G
DARN. I WAS GOING TO ASK YOU FOR POINTERS ABOUT MY SERVICE WEAPON. OH, WELL, I GUESS WE CAN DO THAT AFTER SCHOOL.
YOUR SERVICE--

BY THE WAY, DID YOU KNOW THAT ONE DIANA LANGTON IS MISSING?
WHO?
THE LADY AT K-SQUARE. SHE HASN'T BEEN AT WORK FOR ALMOST A WEEK NOW. I THINK CHARLES TOOK HER AWAY.
HE DID? HOW DID YOU FIND OUT?
TWO OF HIS PALS WERE LOCKED IN THE OLD "SAM'S SWAP SHOP" BUILDING. I WAS THERE WHEN THEY WERE RELEASED AND QUESTIONED.
OH, MAN. I FORGOT ABOUT THEM. WERE THEY OKAY?
YOU FORGOT--
HEY... WHAT'S THAT?
...AND I'LL SUE THE SCHOOL FOR MILLIONS! YOU'LL NEVER WORK IN THIS STATE AGAIN! YOU'LL--

SNAP!
SNAP!
SNAP!
BE MORE UNSTABLE! C'MON, BE MORE UNSTABLE!
AN ALIEN!
A REAL ONE?!
DO YOU WANT TO HANDLE THIS, OR SHOULD I?
YOU CAN HANDLE--?
THANKS! YOU WON'T REGRET IT!
ALIEN INVADER! I'M CECIL HOLMES OF THE BUREAU OF ALIEN MONITORING.
YOU ARE HEREBY ORDERED TO STAND DOWN AND TURN YOURSELF OVER FOR QUESTIONING.
WILL YOU COMPLY?

I DIDN'T THINK SO.
FZZARK!

WHA--? YOU...
THE BUREAU DIDN'T GIVE ME ANY KIND OF CONTAINMENT UNIT, SO I USED AN OLD OLIVE JAR. DO YOU THINK THIS RACE ALLERGIC TO OLIVES? I'D HATE FOR IT TO DISSOLVE INTO GOO BEFORE IT CAN BE STUDIED.
DEEDLE-DEET! DEEDLE-DEET! DEEDLE-DEET! DEEDLE-DEET!
HELLO? YES, SIR. I SHRANK AN ALIEN.
OF COURSE, PLEASE STAND BY.
CLICK!
IT WAS A LOT BIGGER, OF COURSE.
REALLY, SIR? AN UNKNOWN SPECIES? WOW! DO I GET TO NAME IT?
OF COURSE, I'LL ACCEPT WHATEVER DECISION THE BUREAU MAKES, SIR. I'LL FILE A SUGGESTION RIGHT AWAY!
WHAT? OH, YES, HE'S HERE. HANG ON.
THE DIRECTOR WANTS TO TALK TO YOU.
B.A.M.
UH, HELLO?
HELLO, TYLER. WHAT DO YOU THINK OF YOUR CO-AGENT'S SHRINK RAY?
MY CO-AGENT... WAIT... IS THIS--?

I APPOINTED
MYSELF THE "DIRECTOR"
OF THE BUREAU OF ALIEN
NITORING. CECIL'S A PRETTY
ARP KID, AND I THOUGHT "THE
BUREAU" WAS TOO GOOD
AN IDEA TO LET IT
GO TO WASTE.
I CONFISCATED HIS SHRINK-GUN FROM A GUY CALLED **"THE DIMINUTIZER."** HE WAS GOING TO MINIATURIZE A BUNCH OF NBA BASKETBALL PLAYERS AND HOLD THEM FOR RANSOM.
ANYWAY, IT'S PRETTY HARMLESS, AND MOST LEVEL FIVE INTELLECTS CAN **REVERSE** THE PROCESS.
HOW SMART IS A LEVEL FIVE?
HERSCHEL IS A LEVEL NINE.
OH.
BUT... AREN'T YOU AFRAID HE MIGHT... USE IT BADLY?
HE'S **VERY** RESPONSIBLE.
AND I'M ALERTED **EVERY** TIME
E USES IT. BESIDES, I'VE GIVEN
YOU SOME QUITE DESTRUCTIVE
DEVICES, TOO.
I'VE NEVER BEEN A BIG BELIEVER IN THOSE AGE-APPROPRIATE LABELS ON TOYS, YOU KNOW.
OH.
AY. SO... NOW
WHAT?
I'D TAKE THE ALIEN INTO CUSTODY.
INTO--?
THEN GIVE IT TO THE TEACHERS.
BUT--
TAP! TAP!
I GOTTA GO. I THINK I HAVE TO EXPLAIN SOMETHING.
POSITRON SAYS THE CAMERA FEED WENT **NUTS**, SO KEEP AN EYE PEELED FOR THAT THING'S **SLIMY HIDE.**
SHODDY, SHODDY, SHODDY.
YOUR INVASION PLANS ARE **DOOMED!** I DON'T CARE HOW MANY TENTACLES OR GUNS YOUR ALLIES HAVE, WE'LL BEAT YOU ALL!

NO WONDER THIS PLACE GETS SO MUCH ATTENTION FROM WASHINGTON. DO YOU ALWAYS GO OUT IN THE OPEN WITH DEVICES LIKE THAT?
AGENT BAIN, THIS IS... ER...
WE... THERE WAS THIS THING THAT SHOWED UP ON THE SCREENS...
WITH TENTACLES. AND...
WASHINGTON? D.C.?
WHO ARE YOU?
AGENT HOLMES, BUREAU OF ALIEN MONITORING. THANK YOU FOR ALL YOUR WORK MONITORING THE ACTIVITIES OF THESE... BEINGS.
I'M SURE YOU GET OUR REPORTS REGULARLY?
I HAVE NO IDEA WHAT YOU'RE TALKING ABOUT.
OH, RIGHT. IT'S SECRET. SORRY ABOUT THAT.
ANYWAY, I ASSUME YOU'RE AUTHORIZED TO TAKE CUSTODY OF THIS CRIMINAL INVADER?
UNLESS MY PARTNER OBJECTS?
OH, NO. GETTING RID OF IT WOULD BE GREAT.
KEEP UP THE GOOD WORK, SIR.
AND WE'RE WATCHING YOU.
C'MON, TYLER. WE'RE LATE FOR CLASS.

I DON'T KNOW WHAT KIND OF SCHOOL YOU THINK YOU'RE RUNNING HERE...
ME, NEITHER, LATELY...
...BUT YOU'RE GETTING A PERMANENT LIASON TO THE DEPARTMENT OF METAHUMAN AFFAIRS.
WHAT? WHY?
IT'S OBVIOUS THAT CRANSTON CAN'T KEEP THIS PLACE FROM FALLING APART, BLOWING ITS COVER OR LOSING STUDENTS.
CHARLES BRIGMAN WASN'T A STUDENT OF OURS.
AND WE HAVE REPORTS THAT AN UNKOWN PARTY TOOK HIM, SO--
WE SHOULD HAVE ASSIGNED ONE FROM THE BEGINNING, BUT FRANKLY, WE THOUGHT PS238 WOULD HAVE IMPLODED BY NOW.
IT'S ALREADY BEEN DECIDED. YOU'LL GET A DETAILED MEMO BY TOMORROW.
MR. CLAY? I TRUST YOU DO METALWORK?
YOU COULD SAY IT'S A HOBBY. WHY?
SHAME TO LET THIS BAT GO TO WASTE...
SHUSH!
BECAUSE YOU NEED TO TAKE RESPONSIBILITY FOR THE ACTIONS OF ONE OF YOUR STUDENTS. PLEASE FOLLOW ME TO THE PARKING LOT.
PUT THE ZAP GUNS AWAY, FIRST. YOU CAN BRING THE BAT, IF YOU WISH.
OH, RIGHT. SORRY...
I'M SURE HE MEANT THE BAT WASN'T AN OBJECT THAT WOULD AROUSE SUSPICION.
ARE YOU SURE? IT SOUNDED LIKE AN INVITATION TO ME.

EARLIER TODAY, I INTERVIEWED WITH THE PETERSON BOY FOR MY INVESTIGATION INTO THE BRIGMAN INCIDENT.
IF YOU'RE GOING TO TALK TO STUDENTS, YOU REALLY SHOULD CLEAR IT WITH-
ATLAS' SON WASN'T VERY FORTHCOMING. IN FACT, HE WAS DOWNRIGHT DISRESPECTFUL. NOW, I'M SURE YOU'LL FIND THIS HILARIOUS, BUT TO THOSE OF US THAT GREW UP A LONG TIME AGO...
...WE DON'T THINK THIS SORT OF VANDALISM IS AMUSING.
DOES THAT DENT HAVE A SHAPE RESEMBLING, PERHAPS, A MUSICAL INSTRUMENT OWNED BY ONE OF YOUR STUDENTS?
NOW THAT YOU MENTION--
AND NEED I REMIND YOU THAT DAMAGING A GOVERNMENT VEHICLE CAN BE PROSECUTED AS A FEDERAL OFFENSE?
YEAH, I HEARD THAT ONCE OR--
CRANSTON, I'LL EXPECT MY REPLACEMENT RENTAL CAR TO BE HERE BEFORE FIVE.
HAVE THIS CAR REPAIRED AND DELIVERED TO THE DEPARTMENT OF METAHUMAN AFFAIRS MOTOR POOL BY THE END OF THIS MONTH, AND RON PETERSON WON'T HAVE TO SHOW UP IN FRONT OF A JUDGE.
GREAT...

"Analyzing what you haven't got as well as what you have is a necessary ingredient of a career."

- Orison Swett Marden

AARON WILLIAMS'
PS238
TM
DG
DO GOODER PRESS
23
$2.99

PS238
THE SCHOOL FOR METAPRODIGY CHILDREN
BY AARON WILLIAMS

HEY, JULIE.
HI, TYLER! UH... I DIDN'T KNOW YOU HAD A COSTUME... MOSTLY.
YEAH. MY PARENTS MADE ME BRING IT TO PS238. IT GOT...KIND OF MESSED UP. THE HAT AND CAPE WERE THE ONLY PARTS THAT WEREN'T SO DENTED THEY HURT TO WEAR.
DENTED?
I WORE IT TO GYM CLASS.
OH?
IT WAS KIND OF A BAD DAY.
SO IF YOU DON'T HAVE SUPERPOWERS, WHY ARE YOU GOING TO CAREER DAY?
MY MOM AND DAD SAID I STILL MIGHT GET THEM SOMEDAY, SO I HAVE TO GO. I'M SUPPOSED TO "NETWORK."
WHAT'S THAT MEAN?
I THINK IT MEANS YOU TRY TO MAKE FRIENDS WITH PEOPLE SO THEY DO SOMETHING NICE FOR YOU SOMEDAY, LIKE GIVE YOU A JOB.
ISN'T THAT WHAT FRIENDS ARE SUPPOSED TO DO?
YEAH, BUT THE WAY MY MOM SAID IT MADE IT SOUND LIKE IT WAS CHEATING.
TODAY.
Working Heroes Sharing their Experiences
If your parents have had conflicts with any of o guests, please don't bring it up. Inform a teach and you will be escorted to another speaker.

AT LEAST IT'S SOME TIME OUT OF CLASS, RIGHT?
I GUESS-- WOW...
a Decade
We want YOUR Genius!
Meta Tech
Making the Future super!
I DIDN'T THINK THERE WERE THIS MANY SUPERHEROES *ANYWHERE*.
JULIE! TYLER! OVER HERE!
Science Sentinels
METAMESSENGER
FROM PARIS TO PARALLEL

I'VE GOT THE PROGRAM LIST FOR THE COMPANIES, TEAMS, TRAINING CENTERS, AND OTHER GROUPS FOR YOU TO INTERVIEW.
BE SURE TO VISIT WITH AT LEAST A DOZEN OF THEM AND HAVE THEM STAMP YOUR **CAREER COURSE CARD**, OKAY?
PS238
THANKS FOR TREKKING TO PS238!
THANKS, MISTER ALLOY.
WHAT'S THIS PART CIRCLED IN **RED?**
OH, THAT! THAT'S A **SPECIAL GUEST** WE HAVE TODAY! YOU DON'T **HAVE** TO VISIT HIM, BUT I THINK YOU MIGHT GET A **KICK** OUT OF SEEING **WHO** IT **IS!**
PS238
TAKE ME BACK TO MY DORM! I'M IN NO CONDITION TO BE OUT IN **PUBLIC** LIKE **THIS!**
STOP MOANIN'. YOU CHECK OUT **FINE!**
BY **WHOSE** STANDARDS? A ROAD MANAGER FOR SOMEONE WITH A **JEWELRY STORE** EMBEDDED IN THEIR **TEETH?**
TELL YOU WHAT, I'LL ACTIVATE YOUR **HOLOGRAM**, HOW'S THAT?
YOU JUST DO THAT.
PIK!
VORP!
THE HOLOGRAM TEMPLATE'S SUPPOSED TO BE **ENCRYPTED.**
GO FIGURE. YOU WANT TO LET ANGIE AND THE "ILLEGAL ALIEN" TAKE A WHACK AT THE NEXT **SCHOOL NETWORK UPDATE**, TOO?

TITTER! HEE-HEE! CHORTLE! SHH! SNRK! HEEHEEHEE!
THIS, THIS IS THE MULCH I'VE HAD TO ENDURE FOR ALMOST A WEEK! BUT DOES ANYONE CARE? NO! I GET YET ANOTHER DAY OF DROWNING IN OTHERS' STUPIDITY WHILE WEARING CHROME EXHAUST PIPES OR VELVET AND LEOPARD SKIN!
HAHAHAHAHAHAHAHAH
AND DID YOU LISTEN? OH, NO. MY PLEAS FOR RELIEF WENT UNANSWERED. "WE-UN'S GONNA BE FEUDIN' WITH ALIENS" OR SOME OTHER GUMMI BEAR EXCUSE!
KNOW, SIR, THAT YOU'VE MADE MANKIND'S DESTINY A VELOURLOAD WORSE!
AND IF YOU DON'T GET THIS BASS CANNON OUT OF MY CHAIR BY SUNDOWN, YOU'D BETTER GET READY TO POP FOR SPINAL SURGERY!
OOM-BOOM BAM! BA-BOOM-BOOM BAM! BA-BOOM-BOOM BAM!
THAT-- SNORT! --WAS THE GREATEST THING-- CHOKE! EVER!
HEE-HEE-HEE! I--GASP!--I ALMOST PEED MYSELF! HEEHEEHEEHEE HEEHEE!
I DON'T WANNA DO THIS.
YOU DON'T HAVE TO DO ANYTHING HARD. JUST LISTEN TO WHAT THEY HAVE TO SAY. WHO KNOWS? YOU MIGHT FIND SOMETHING YOU WANT TO PURSUE. AND THERE'S FUN SURPRISE AT THE RED CIRCLE, THERE. I THINK YOU'LL REALLY LIKE IT!
AS SOON AS MISS KYLE COMES TO TAKE OVER GREETING EVERYONE, I'M HEADED THERE MYSELF!
OKAY... WHERE DO I GO FIRST?
WHEREVER YOU WANT. JUST HAVE THEM STAMP YOUR CARD.
OKAY.

UH, CAPTIAN CLARINET? WAIT UP!
HI, TYLER. WHAT DO YOU WANT?
I JUST WANTED TO SEE, UM, WHO YOU WERE GOING TO TALK TO?
OH. WELL... DO YOU WANT TO SEE WHO'S IN THE RED CIRCLE?
I DON'T CARE, REALLY.
IT'S A STAMP CLOSER TO LEAVING, SO SURE.
OH-KAY... I THINK IT'S UP HERE, TO THE RIGHT...
HEAD'S UP!
OH, HI, JULIE!
BOING!

HEROIX
HEY, KIDS! I'M VICTORIOUS, AND I WORK FOR HEROIX, INCORPORATED, A MULTINATIONAL COMPANY THAT EMPLOYS MORE METAHUMANS THAN ANY OTHER FOR-PROFIT ORGANIZATION ON EARTH!
WHAT THAT MEANS IS, IF SOMEONE NEEDS A HERO FOR ANY REASON, HEROIX GIVES YOU A CALL, AND YOU GET TO SAVE THE DAY! DOESN'T THAT SOUND LIKE FUN?
BUT IT'S NOT ALL SAVING THE DAY, IS IT?
WHAT'S THAT, SON?
I HAVE SUBSTANTIAL STOCK HOLDINGS IN HEROIX. WHILE IT HAS A STABLE OF HERO-TYPES THAT DOES DO WORK-FOR-HIRE THAT COULD BE CALLED "SAVING THE DAY," MOST OF IT IS ONLY A STEP UP FROM DRESSING IN A CLOWN COSTUME FOR BIRTHDAY PARTIES, ISN'T IT?
UH... WHAT'S YOUR NAME, KID?
VICTOR VON FOGG. BUT YOU CAN CALL ME BY MY NICKNAME, "THE GUY WHO COULD GET YOU FIRED."
SO WHAT WAS THE LAST JOB YOU DID, THE ONE BEFORE THEY ASKED YOU TO LIFT METAL BRICKS FOR OUR AMUSEMENT?
ER, I SIGNED A NON-DISCLOSURE AGREEMENT, SO--
THOSE AREN'T WORTH THE PAPER THEY'RE PRINTED ON. SO THINK OF YOUR NEXT PERFORMANCE EVALUATION, AND TELL US ABOUT YOUR MOST RECENT SUPER-TEMP JOB.
I... UM... I...

...I DRESSED AS "THE TIRE TITAN" FOR THE GRAND OPENING OF A FULL-SERVICE CAR CARE FRANCHISE IN EL PASO.
SO SIGN UP, EVERYONE! A LIFE OF LOCAL TV AWAITS YOU!
AHHH... THAT KIND OF SATISFACTION IS WORTH A TWO-POINT DIP IN THE STOCK PRICE...
UH... MISTER? MISTER VICTORIOUS?
HI, LITTLE LADY. DO YOU WANT YOUR STAMP? I MEAN, I KNOW THE TALK WASN'T MUCH, BUT...
WHAT ARE YOUR POWERS? YOU CAN FLY AND YOU'RE STRONG, RIGHT?
YEAH. FLIGHT, INVULNERABLE, STRENGTH, SPEED. IT'S NOTHING ALL THAT SPECIAL, IF YOU--
WHAT'S YOUR NUMBER?
WHAT?
YOUR NUMBER. SOMEONE SAID YOU HAD A NUMBER BECAUSE OF YOUR POWERS, DIDN'T THEY?

I'M THE SEVENTY-FIRST.
EIGHTY-FOURTH.
GOOD LUCK, KID.
YOU, TOO.
HEY, THERE.
WHAT WOULD YOU THINK IF I HAD A BUNCH OF GNATS DECIDE TO HAVE A HOUSE PARTY IN VONFOGG'S ARMOR?
YOU'D DO THAT FOR ME?
I'D LOVE IT. THANKS!
I'D DO IT ANYWAY. I JUST WANTED TO KNOW WHAT YOU THOUGHT.
NO PROBLEM. WILL YOU WANT PICTURES? I BROUGHT A CAMERA.
MEANWHILE...
I THINK IT'S RIGHT OVER HERE.
IT'S PROBABLY MISTER ALLOY'S OLD SUPER-TEAM OR SOMETHING.
I DON'T THINK SO. I RAN INTO HIM LAST WEEK, AND HE WAS REALLY EXCITED ABOUT...
THAT GUY!
HE LOOKS KINDA FAMILIAR.
DON'T YOU WATCH "STAR TREK?" C'MON!
Wil Wheat
representing the Metahuman Screen
Special Effects Guild, and Set Constr
THANKS FOR TREKKING TO PS238!

...AND EVEN IF I DIDN'T HAVE TELEKINETIC POWERS, I WOULD STILL HAVE GONE INTO ACTING. IT'S A GREAT FIELD, AND YOU MEET ALL KINDS OF INTERESTING AND AMAZING PEOPLE.
HAVE ANY OF YOU SEEN ME ON TV?
I HAVE! YOU DRIVE THE SPACESHIP!
THAT'S RIGHT. BUT I DID A LOT MORE ON THE SET.
REMEMBER WHEN YOU SAW SPACESHIPS ORBITING PLANETS OR FIGHTING EACH OTHER?
BEING TELEKINETIC MEANS I CAN MOVE THINGS WITH MY MIND. I OPENED THE SLIDING DOORS, MADE SPACESHIPS FLY, AND HELPED TOSS ACTORS AWAY FROM PRETEND EXPLOSIONS.
MY AGENT ONLY REMEMBERED TO HAVE ME GET PAID FOR THE ACTING PART, SO DON'T BE LIKE HIM: STAY IN SCHOOL.
ANYWAY, ACTING ISN'T ALL THERE IS TO THE ENTERTAINMENT INDUSTRY.
IF YOU'RE GOOD AT MAKING UP STORIES, YOU COULD ALSO FIND YOURSELF WRITING FOR MOVIES, TV SHOWS, AND EVEN COMIC BOOKS.
ZAP!
I'VE DONE VOICE ACTING FOR A LOT OF CARTOON SHOWS, AND I'M EVEN WRITING A STORY FOR A COMIC BOOK ABOUT A CHARACTER I PLAYED ON TELEVISION.
NEAT, HUH?
BOOM!

SO IF YOU CAN MEMORIZE WORDS REALLY WELL, AND MAKE PEOPLE FEEL WHAT YOU FEEL--
I CAN DO THAT! WANNA SEE? I GOT THESE FERRA... PHONO... PHONEAMOANS?
--WHEN THEY SEE YOU, YOU MIGHT WANT TO TRY OUT FOR A FEW SCHOOL PLAYS. WHO KNOWS? YOU MIGHT JUST FIND YOURSELF IN HOLLYWOOD SOMEDAY!
SO IF YOU WANT TO COME UP TO THE TABLE, I'LL STAMP YOUR CARDS AND ANSWER ANY QUESTIONS YOU HAVE.
AHEM...
AND I'LL AUTOGRAPH ANY POSTERS YOU MIGHT HAVE HAPPENED TO BRING TO SCHOOL.
WHAT DO YOU DO IF YOU CAN'T DO MUCH OF ANYTHING?
BASED ON MY EXPERIENCE, YOU BECOME A SCRIPTWRITER OR A PRODUCER.
IS THAT GOOD?
DEPENDS ON WHO HAS TO WORK WITH YOU.
WHY DIDN'T YOU BECOME A SUPERHERO INSTEAD?
BECAUSE "TELEKINETIC BOY" JUST DIDN'T SOUND RIGHT. REALLY, I DIDN'T THINK I WAS CUT OUT FOR IT.
AND YOUR PARENTS WEREN'T UPSET?
OH, NO. THE FLOATING SILVERWARE TRICK DIDN'T COME WITH THE BULLETPROOF BODY TRICK.
PLUS, I CAN'T LEVITATE MYSELF FOR SOME REASON, AND MY SCHWINN DIDN'T MAKE A GOOD "WHEATON MOBILE."
WEHATON, YOUR LEVITATION SHENANIGANS SET COMPUTER-GENERATED SPECIAL EFFECTS BACK TEN YEARS.
THIS FLASH DRIVE CONTAINS FILES DETAILING EVERY OTHER WAY YOU MADE STAR TREK STINK.
BA-BOOM-BOOM BAM! BA-BOOM-BOO

I'M REALLY SORRY ABOUT THAT, MISTER WHEATON.
NO PROBLEM. THESE WILL COME IN HANDY FOR MY REVIEWS OF THE TREK DVDS.
WANT ANOTHER POSTER SIGNED?
WELL... YOU'VE ALREADY DONE SO MANY FOR ME...
IT'S NO TROUBLE. CHECK THIS OUT: IT'S A NEW AUTOGRAPHING TRICK I'VE WORKED UP.
IT TOOK A LOT OF PRACTICE TO GET IT RIGHT; I THINK MY POWERS ARE RIGHT-HANDED.
THAT... WAS THE MOST BEAUTIFUL THING I'VE EVER SEEN.
YOU SHOULD WATCH WHAT I CAN DO WITH "GUITAR HERO."
HI, THERE! I LIKE YOUR HELMET!
IT WAS FORGED BY ZEUS!
YOU DON'T SAY...
WHERE DO YOU GUYS WANT TO GO NEXT?
THIS IS BORING. I DIDN'T THINK SUPERHEROES COULD BE THIS BORING.
THOSE PEOPLE DON'T LOOK BORING. THEY LOOK KIND OF SCARY.

PRAETORIAN ACADEMY
WOW. I DIDN'T KNOW THERE WERE OTHER SCHOOLS LIKE OURS.
I NEED ANOTHER STAMP. LET'S GO.
I DON'T CARE FOR THEIR PHILOSOPHY. IT SEEMS TO BENEFIT THE SCHOOL MORE THAN IT DOES THE STUDENT.
WE HAD TO OPEN CAREER DAY TO EVERY ORGANIZATION. UNLESS THEY ADVOCATE BREAKING THE LAW, DISCRIMINATION, OR OVERT GLOBAL DOMINATION, THEY CAN SET UP SHOP JUST LIKE EVERYONE ELSE.
I DON'T SEE ANYTHING OVERT IN THEIR PAMPHLET, BUT...
IT READS JUST ABOUT LIKE EVERY OTHER CORPORATE BROCHURE; BE THE BIGGEST AND THE BEST, BEAT THE COMPETITION...
BUT THIS STUFF HERE ABOUT SUPERIORITY AND SERVING CLIENTS NATIONALLY AND INTERNATIONALLY. IT'S SOUNDING A LOT LIKE YOU COULD HIRE OUT YOUR OWN META-ARMY.
MERCENARY WORK BY METAS ISN'T THAT UNCOMMON, BUT IT DOESN'T TEND TO PAY OFF IN THE LONG RUN FOR A COUNTRY BECAUSE IT'S HARD TO PLAN MILITARY CAMPAIGNS AROUND SUPERPOWERS: YOU CAN SUDDENLY LOSE THEM BECAUSE YOUR FREELANCER GETS A BETTER OFFER OR YOUR ENEMY HIRES ONE, TOO.
OUR OWN MILITARY DOESN'T TRAIN METAHUMANS FOR COMBAT UNLESS THEY'RE WILLING TO LEAVE THE CAPE IN THE BARRACKS.
COULDN'T ONE CITE DISCRIMINATION BASED ON THEIR SELECTION PROCESS? THEY HAVE A STRICT METAHUMANS-ONLY POLICY.
IT'S NOT LIKE WE DON'T HAVE THE SOMETHING SIMILAR. IT'S IN THE APPLICATION FORMS: NO STUDENT CAN BE ADMITTED TO PS238 IF THEY DON'T POSSESS ANY--
OH, HELLO, TYLER!

WHAT? OH, HI, MRS. OBERON.
WHAT ABOUT THE "SUPER SEARCH AND RESCUE" PEOPLE TWO BOOTHS OVER? WE CAN GO THERE INSTEAD. THEY LOOK A LOT MORE--
STOP BEING SUCH A FRAIDY-CAT ABOUT IT. C'MON.
YOU'RE GOING TO THE PRAETORIAN BOOTH, TYLER?
I GUESS SO. IS THERE SOMETHING WRONG WITH THEM?
IT'S JUST... ER...
I GUESS "MOTHERLY CONCERN" ISN'T A GOOD REASON...
GO AND GET YOUR STAMP, SON.
OH. OKAY.
ALFRED, WHAT ARE YOU--?
IT'S JUST A STAMP, MS. IMPERIA.

WHY ARE WE MAKING HIM ATTEND THIS EVENT IN THE FIRST PLACE?
HIS PARENTS **INSISTED.**
NOW, IF THE PRAETORIANS DO ANYTHING **UN-PLEASANT** TO HIM, THEN YOU MIGHT HAVE GROUNDS FOR A **COMPLAINT.**
IF NOT, WELL, WE HAVE **COMPETITION** FOR STUDENTS, WHICH MIGHT NOT BE A **BAD** THING.
EXCUSE US, WE COULDN'T HELP OVERHEARING...
MRS. OBERON? PRINCIPAL CRANSTON?
UNDER THE FREEDOM OF INFORMATION ACT, WE'D LIKE TO SEE **PS238'S APPLICATION FORMS,** AT YOUR EARLIEST CONVENIENCE.
NOW WOULD BE GOOD.

MEANWHILE...
...AND PRAETORIAN ACADEMY IS FIRST AND FOREMOST ABOUT EXCELLENCE.
YOU LEARN DISCIPLINE, CONTROL, AND CONFIDENCE.
IT SOUNDS KIND OF... STRICT.
THAT'S THE POINT. WE ARE LIKE LIONS AMONG MEN. WE MUST KNOW WHEN IT IS RIGHT AND CORRECT TO USE OUR POWERS, BOTH FOR CIVILIZATION'S BENEFIT AND FOR OURS.
UNDER THE PRAETORIAN ORDER, YOU KNOW WHAT IS EXPECTED OF YOU AT ALL TIMES.
YOU GUYS ARE LIONS?
WOW. YOU ALWAYS KNOW WHAT TO DO?
BUT... WHAT IF I DON'T WANT TO BE... SUPER WHEN I GROW UP?
ALL GRADUATES OF PRAETORIAN ACADEMY WILL HAVE A PLACE AND A PURPOSE FOR THE REST OF THEIR LIVES.
GOVERNMENT
PRIVATE SECTOR
YOU CAN GROW RICH, IF THAT IS YOUR GOAL, SERVE HUMANITY, OR DO WHATEVER YOU WANT.
RESEARCH
DEMOLITION
INTELLIGENCE
ENTERTAINMENT
OUR PROGRAM IS THERE TO MAKE SURE THAT YOU CAN DO WHAT YOU DO BEST.
THAT SOUNDS... GOOD, I GUESS.
HERE ARE YOUR STAMPS. TAKE SOME OF OUR BOOKLETS. IF YOU DECIDE YOU'D LIKE TO KNOW MORE, HAVE YOUR PARENTS CALL THE NUMBER ON THE BACK, OR THEY CAN CONTACT US ON METANET.
THANKS. I'LL SHOW THIS TO THEM. I MEAN, HER.
HOW WAS IT?
IT WAS... NOT BORING.
THEY STILL GIVE ME THE SPOOKIES.

REALLY? WHAT DID THEY SAY?
THAT WE GOTTA BE **BETTER** THAN NORMAL PEOPLE IF WE WANT TO USE OUR **POWERS** AND STUFF.
BUT YOU WOULDN'T WANT TO GO TO A **DIFFERENT SCHOOL,** WOULD YOU, TYLER?
IT'D BE UP TO **HIM.**
I THINK HE SHOULD HEAR ABOUT OUR SCHOOL.
UH, I DON'T--
IT'S JUST A **TALK** AND SOME **PAPERS.** AND YOU GET THROUGH ANOTHER **STAMP.**
SO LET'S **GO.**
YEAH, BUT I--
JUST COME OVER TO THE **BOOTH.** I CAN TELL YOU ALL ABOUT IT.
UNDER-GUARD GREYHOUND! WHAT ARE YOU **DOING?**
JUST TELLING THIS KID ABOUT OUR, UH, SUPERIOR--
YOU CAN DO THAT BEHIND OUR BOOTH'S **TABLE,** CAN'T YOU, UNDERGUARD GREYHOUND?
SURE, UM, PRAETORIAN ONYX.
THEN LEAVE HIM BE AND FOLLOW ME. **AFTER** YOU **APOLOGIZE.**

I... APOLOGIZE... FOR... GETTING IN YOUR FACE.
IT'S OKAY. I--
IF YOU WANT TO COME HEAR ABOUT OUR SCHOOL... YOU CAN. IF YOU DON'T, IT'S YOUR LOSS.
SHAKE?
SEE? THEY'RE SPOOKY.
SO'S ZODON.
THIS PRAETORIAN PLACE JUST SENT THE WRONG GUY TO HELP WITH THEIR BOOTH.
SURE. UM... CAN I HAVE MY HAND BACK, NOW?
I ONLY NEED A FEW MORE STAMPS AND I'M DONE.
WAIT, TYLER DIDN'T GET ONE.
HEY, TYLER, WHERE DO YOU WANT TO--?
WHERE'D HE GO?
PROBABLY TO THE BATHROOM. WHO CARES?
LET'S JUST PICK ANOTHER BOOTH AND GET THIS OVER WITH.
CAPTAIN? JULIE?

SORRY TO BOTHER YOU KIDS, BUT IS TYLER WITH YOU? OR IS HE STILL OVER AT THE PRAETORIAN BOOTH?
I GUESS HE COULD BE. JEEPERS, WHY DON'T YOU PEOPLE MAKE HIM CARRY A FLAG IF HE'S SO IMPORTANT?!
I DON'T THINK SO. THAT ONE PURTORIA GUY WAS KINDA MEAN TO HIM.
WHAT ONE PRAETORIAN GUY?
HE WAS WANTING TO TALK WITH TYLER, BUT TYLER DIDN'T WANT TO GO WITH HIM. THEN HE GRABBED TYLER'S CAPE AND TRIED TO DRAG HIM TO THEIR BOOTH.
THEY WANTED TO INTERVIEW HIM?
PRINCIPAL CRANSTON!
WE'VE READ OVER THE PS238 APPLICATION FORMS, AND WE NEED TO TALK WITH YOU IMMEDIATELY.
OUR VERY SYSTEM OF DEMOCRACY IS AT STAKE.
THIS ISN'T ABOUT FLUORIDE IN THE WATER AGAIN, IS IT?

NO. ACCORDING TO BLOCK FIVE, PAGE TWO, UNDER THE HEADING OF "METAHUMAN ABILITIES, CHECK ALL THAT APPLY," THERE'S A WORD THAT CAUGHT OUR INTEREST.
"REQUIRED."
IF ONE DOESN'T HAVE POWERS, WE SUBMIT THAT THEY CANNOT BE CONSIDERED A STUDENT AT PS238.
AND IF ONE ISN'T OFFICIALLY A STUDENT, ONE CANNOT HOLD THE OFFICE OF CLASS PRESIDENT.
WHICH IS CURRENTLY OCCUPIED BY TYLER MARLOCKE.
ILLEGALLY.
WELL... HANG ON, HIS CASE WAS GIVEN SPECIAL CONSIDERATION BECAUSE HIS PARENTS ARE--
OH, WHAT A SAD DAY IT IS WHEN DEMOCRACY IS THWARTED BY WHO YOU'RE RELATED TO.
I THINK I FEEL MY EVERY NOTION OF WHAT MADE THIS COUNTRY GREAT TURNING TO DUST.
I KNOW MY FAITH IN OUR CONSTITUTION IS BEING SHAKEN AT THIS VERY MOMENT.
IT'S LIKE THE FOUNDING FATHERS' SIGNATURES ARE SLIDING RIGHT OFF THE PARCHMENT.
I THINK I FEEL THE COLD DRAFT OF TYRANNY SLIPPING THROUGH--
THAT'S ENOUGH! YOU'VE MADE YOUR POINT. CAN WE AT LEAST FINISH CAREER DAY BEFORE WE START IMPEACHING CLASSMATES?
ILLEGAL CLASSMATES.
SPEAKING OF WHOM, WHERE IS OUR PRESIDENT-IN-NAME-ONLY? I THOUGHT HE WAS AROUND HERE.

"I'M SURE HE'LL SHOW UP SOON ENOUGH SO YOU CAN TELL HIM THE GOOD NEWS, PATRIOT."
"IT'S NEVER GOOD NEWS WHEN DEMOCRACY IS SUBVERTED, AS YOU WELL--"
"THANK YOU, EAGLE. DON'T YOU TWO HAVE CARDS TO GET STAMPED? I THINK DEMOCRACY CAN SURVIVE ANOTHER DAY OR TWO..."
"...AND I DON'T THINK TYLER NEEDS ANY MORE ANXIETY FOR TODAY, ALL RIGHT?"
CLASS DISMISSED!
PS238

"Man must rise above the Earth, to the top of the atmosphere and beyond, for only thus will he fully understand the world in which he lives."

- *Socrates*

"But you're not to fly down low again and try to read the signposts. Every time you do that, humans rush into the streets and we get lots of shouting on the radio."

- *Terry Pratchett*

AARON WILLIAMS'
PS238
TM
DG
DO GOODER PRESS
24
$2.99
Taken from earth...
...left on a rock floating in eternity...
...and it's not even lunchtime yet.
WWW.PS238.COM
DGP024 • ISBN# 978-1-933288-30-7
50299
9 781933 288307

PS238
THE SCHOOL FOR METAPRODIGY CHILDREN
BY AARON WILLIAMS
I WAS AT CAREER DAY...
...AT SCHOOL...
...SHAKING HANDS WITH THAT CREEPY GUY IN BLACK...
...NOW I'M WHEREVER THIS PLACE IS...
...AND I DON'T KNOW HOW I GOT HERE.
THIS IS PROBABLY NOT GOOD.
I SHOULD LEAVE, SOMEHOW. AND SOON.
HELLO? IS ANYONE HERE?
HOW DO I GO HOME?
YOU DON'T.

THIS IS YOUR HOME FOREVER. FOR YOU AND EVERY OTHER WIMPWEED I DECIDE TO GET RID OF!
THE ONLY THING I WANT OUTTA YOU...
...ASIDE FROM YEARS OF BEGGIN' ME TO LET YOU SEE EARTH FOR EVEN FIVE MINUTES...
...IS WHAT'S A WUSSY LIKE YOU DOIN' IN A SCHOOL FULL OF SUPER-WEENIES?
I... I...
MAYBE IF YOU SAW WHO YOU WERE TALKIN' TO...
...YOU'D GET SCARED ENOUGH TO TALK!
CHARLES?! WHUH-- YOU--
WHAT WERE YOU DOING AT THAT PS238 PLACE?
CLUNK!
WHAT KIND OF SUPER- POWER COULD A RUNT LIKE YOU HAVE? LET'S SEE IT SAVE YOUR BUTT FROM A ROYAL POUNDING, TY-D-BOWL!

BEGINING PL*BRZZT*:
ATTENTIONNNZERK!
--ULTIMA POWERS *RZRKRACKLE* MY SON--*BLEEP*
--COSMIC POWER HE *SSSRKKK!* WEILDZZZRT!
--MAKE NO ATTEMPT *PLERRRRBTT*
--I WILL BE FORCED TO SPEAK WITH YOUR SUPERIORS.
END PLAYBACK. HOLO-HELMET REQUIRES SERVICE. PLEASE CONTACT YOUR NEAREST CLAY INDUSTRIES SUPPORT CENTER.
YOU'RE ULTIMA POWERS' KID?!
YOU-- I GOTTA THINK!
HEY, WAIT! IT'S NOT--
WHAT YOU...
AW, POOP.
TYLER? IS THAT YOU?

OH! YOU'RE DIANA, RIGHT? YOU WORK AT K-SQUARE?
RIGHT. I GOT DUMPED HERE A WHILE BACK BY THAT KID YOU AND YOUR FRIENDS CAUGHT SWIPING MY CANDY.
WAS THAT GUY IN BLACK THE SAME KID? I ONLY SAW HIM FOR A SECOND.
YEAH. CHARLES BRIGMAN. BUT HE'S GOT A UNIFORM AND STUFF. HE GOT TAKEN AWAY AND NOW HE LOOKS LIKE HE'S IN THE ARMY OR SOMETHING.
I WONDERED WHY HE STOPPED COMING AROUND HERE. WANT SOMETHING TO EAT? HE DIDN'T LEAVE MUCH VARIETY, BUT HE POPPED MY ENTIRE STOCK OF COSMIC CRUNCH BARS AND A FEW GALLONS OF ATLAS-AIDE SPORTS DRINK TO THIS ROCK.
HOW LONG HAVE YOU BEEN HERE?
A LITTLE OVER TWO WEEKS. IS ANYONE LOOKING FOR ME?
A FRIEND OF MINE IS.
A FRIEND OF YOURS?
CECIL.
IS HE A POLICE OFFICER?
KIND OF. HE'S IN MY MATH CLASS.
OH. GREAT.
WELL, YOU CAN PULL UP A ROCK AND SIT A SPELL. THERE'S NOTHING MUCH TO LOOK AT AROUND HERE, EXCEPT FOR THE LINES ON THE GROUND.
LINES?
YEAH. OVER THERE TO YOUR LEFT.
ATLAS ADE
12 COUNT
COSMIC CRUNCH
12 COUNT
COSM
CRUN

I ALSO FOUND A BASKETBALL. WEIRD, HUH?
YEAH, THAT IS PRETTY... WEIRD.
YOU'RE PROBABLY NOT GOING TO BELIEVE THIS, BUT I THINK I'VE BEEN HERE BEFORE...
BUT I THOUGHT CHARLES COULDN'T REMEMBER IT...
MEANWHILE, BACK ON THE EXCELSIOR SCHOOL PLAYGROUND...
SO LET ME GET THIS STRAIGHT: YOU'RE SUPPOSED TO BE ATTENDING A "CAREER DAY" THING SOMEWHERE, BUT YOU'RE NOT, BUT YOU ARE?
A HOMUNCULUS OF MYSELF IS DOING SO IN MY PLACE.
A HAMA..?
A CONSTRUCT THAT LOOKS LIKE ME AND ACTS LIKE ME. I BUILT IT OUT OF CAFETERIA FOOD. I WAS AMAZED AT HOW READILY IT ANIMATED.
I FIND OUR CURRENT TASK MORE INTERESTING, ANYWAY.

GOOD. OKAY, SO YOU KNOW WHERE WE'RE GOING?
FROM YOUR DESCRIPTION, YES. BUT WITHOUT A FORMAL CHALLENGE TO INVOKE OUR TRANSPORT THERE, WE'LL HAVE TO GO BY THE *LONG ROAD.*
HOW DO WE GET STARTED?
TO BEGIN WITH, WE HAD TO WAIT UNTIL *TODAY* FOR THE PLANES TO ALIGN AS THEY DO EVERY TUESDAY.
WHY TUESDAY?
MOST COSMIC EVENTS HAPPEN ON TUESDAYS.
OH.
AH. I FOUND IT. STEP THROUGH THE PARTING WITH ME.
STEP WHERE?
SIDEWAYS, BETWEEN THE SECONDS, UNDERNEATH THE THIRD AND FIFTH DIMENSIONS.
WOW! IS THIS WHERE YOU'RE FROM?
SOMEPLACE LIKE IT. I AM ALIEN TO YOUR WORLD, BUT NOT FROM OUTER SPACE.
THAT'S EVEN *COOLER!* AND TRAVELING LIKE THIS PROBABLY SAVES ON *DILITHIUM,* HUH?
IT COULD, I SUPPOSE.
SO LONG AS WE REMAIN TRUE TO OUR PATH, THOSE WE ENCOUNTER WON'T BE ABLE TO PERCEIVE US.
YOU WILL KNEEL BEFORE VONFHTAGN!
IN YOUR DREAMS. ZODTHULU WILL CRUSH YOUR PUNY INTELLECT!

WOW. THEY'RE LIKE PHANTOMS!
SO LONG AS WE STAY ON THE PATH, WE HAVE NOTHING TO FEAR. THEY CANNOT SEE OR TOUCH US, AND WE PAST THROUGH THEM LIKE THEY ARE MIST.
BUT SOME OF THEM MIGHT SEE US, RIGHT? I MEAN, THERE ARE PROBABLY OTHER BEINGS LIKE YOU, AREN'T THERE, MALPHAST?
IF THAT HAPPENS, WE MUST NOT LEAD THEM BACK TO YOUR WORLD. VERY OFTEN, SPECIES FROM ONE PLANE DO NOT MIX WELL WITH THOSE OF ANOTHER.
NONE SHALL PASS.
BUT THE REAL THREAT IS THOSE THINGS THAT LIVE IN BETWEEN.
THINGS LIVE ON THIS PATH WE'RE FOLLOWING?
SOME. THEY ARE RARE, BUT NOT UNHEARD OF.
WHAT ARE THEY?
SOME ARE WHAT YOU'D CALL GHOSTS, BUT THE ACCURATE TERM IS "NEVERBORN." OTHERS ARE LEFTOVERS FROM DIMENSIONS THAT HAVE RECEDED.
HOW WILL WE KNOW IF WE SEE ONE?
OH, IT WILL BE QUITE HORRIFIC. IT WILL REMIND YOU OF DEATH, MOST LIKELY.
I SEE. THEN I THINK WE'VE GOT A PROBLEM.

I THINK THIS IS A JOB FOR MY SHRINK RAY.
WE SHOULD RUN INSTEAD, FRIEND CECIL. YOUR TECHNOLOGY PROBABLY WON'T FUNCTION NORMALLY HERE.
WHAT WOULD HAPPEN IF I TRIED IT?
THE RESULTS COULD COLLAPSE SPACE-TIME.
OH. THEN ONLY AS A LAST RESORT?
MAYBE, ONLY IF YOU LOSE SEVERAL LIMBS...

HERE! WE CAN LEAVE THE PATH HERE!
JUMP!
ARE YOU ALL RIGHT, FRIEND CECIL?
I THINK SO...
IT... KIND OF WENT THROUGH ME. NOW MY STOMACH ITCHES...
I SEE. DOES IT HURT?
NO. IT KIND OF TICKLES NOW. AND I THINK I CAN SMELL THROUGH THEM, TOO.
WE HAVE TO TRAVEL WORLD-TO-WORLD NOW, SO WE SHOULD MOVE ON. I'LL SEE ABOUT PUTTING YOU TO RIGHTS LATER.

MEANWHILE, BACK ON THE ROCK...
SO, TYLER. HOW'S LIFE TREATING YOU AT PS238?
UH, WHERE? I DON'T KNOW WHAT A PS238 IS.
YOU DON'T HAVE TO PLAY DUMB WITH ME. I KNOW ALL ABOUT IT.
YOU DO? UH... HOW? YOU WORK AT A QUICKIE MART.
YOU MIGHT SAY I'M DOCTOR POSITRON'S SISTER.
BUT HE'S A ROBOT.
I'VE ALWAYS LIKED THE TERM "ARTIFICIAL AMERICAN." THAT'S POSITRON NUMBER TWO'S JOKE.
YOU'RE A ROB--UH, ARTIFACIAL AMERICAN, TOO?
YEP. I RUN THE K-SQUARE AND KEEP AN EYE ON THINGS IN TOWN. I'M ALSO DOING AN EXPERIMENT ON HUMAN BEHAVIOR, BUT THAT'S JUST A HOBBY.
BESIDES, WHO ELSE BUT AN ANDROID COULD LIVE HERE FOR TWO WEEKS WITHOUT STARVING OR SMELLING LIKE A HAM SANDWICH LEFT IN A HOT CAR FOR A MONTH?
YOU'RE DOING EXPERIMENTS ON THE TOWN?
I'M COMPARING HOW PEOPLE TREAT ME, SINCE I LOOK FEMALE, TO HOW THEY RESPOND TO MY BROTHERS. IT'S JUST SOMETHING TO DO, WHEN I'M BORED.
BUT WHAT I REALLY WANT TO DO IS LEARN ENOUGH ABOUT PEOPLE TO WRITE ROMANCE NOVELS.
YOU DO?

SURE. WHY NOT? DON'T YOU WANT TO DO SOMETHING WITH YOUR LIFE SOMEDAY?
NOT BE HERE.
BESIDES THAT.
MY PARENTS THINK I'LL BE A SUPERHERO.
THE GUYS TELL ME YOU MIGHT HAVE SOME TROUBLE WITH THAT.
YEAH, MOST EVERYONE THINKS SO. BUT I'M WEARING A CAPE, SO--
DIANA INSTANTLY FINDS HERSELF ON THE EDGE OF THE ROCK...
STAY HERE IF YOU KNOW WHAT'S GOOD FOR YOU!
DANGIT! TOO SLOW!
I NEED TO UPGRADE MY SERVOS.

TYLER? KIDDO? ARE YOU OKAY?
ONLY IF I DON'T MOVE...
CHARLES PUT THIS COLLAR AROUND MY NECK. HE SAYS IF I WALK MORE THAN THREE FEET FROM THIS LITTLE METAL THING ON THE GROUND, IT'LL FRY MY HEAD.
IS HE GONE?
I THINK SO. HE'S SUPPOSED TO BE AT PS238'S CAREER DAY. I'LL BET HE'S WORRIED SOMEONE WILL SEE HE'S MISSING.
LET ME TAKE A LOOK AT THAT THING.
POSITRON NUMBER ONE IS THE REAL MECHANIC IN THE FAMILY, BUT WE ALL HAVE A KNACK WITH MACHINES.
CAN YOU GET IT OFF?
I THINK SO. MOST OF MY ACTUAL EXPERIENCE IS WITH SLUSHIE MACHINES, THOUGH.
IS THIS COLLAR LIKE A SLUSHIE MACHINE?

IF IT MAKES YOU FEEL BETTER, SURE. BUT WHY DO YOU MAKE HIM SO NERVOUS?
HE KIND OF FOUND OUT WHO MY PARENTS ARE. HE PROBABLY THINKS I CAN THROW CARS AROUND AND BLAST HOLES IN ROCKS.
HE'S THIS SCARED OF YOU, BUT HE STUCK AROUND TO TELL YOU ABOUT THIS COLLAR?
HE APPEARED, PUT THIS THING ON ME, AND LEFT THIS NOTE ABOUT IT.
AH.
HE DOESN'T SPELL VERY WELL.
NOT SURPRISED...
AT THAT MOMENT, SEVERAL DIMENSIONS AWAY...
THIS IS COOL!
PLEASE, STOP... TOUCHING EVERYTHING, FRIEND CECIL. I DON'T KNOW IF YOUR BODY CAN WITHSTAND MORE CHANGES...
...AND I DON'T WANT FRIEND TYLER TO THINK I CAN'T BE RESPONSIBLE WITH HIS COMPANIONS.
SO WHERE ARE WE NOW?
WE'RE IN A PLACE I PROBABLY SHOULDN'T BE, BUT...
MALPHAST! YOU CAME FOR A VISIT!

BUT YOU'RE VERY FORTUNATE THE LORDS OF CHAOS HAVE THEIR MANY EYES MOSTLY ELSEWHERE. I CAN SHIELD US FOR A SHORT TIME, THOUGH.
IT'S SO WONDERFUL TO SEE YOU, MY SON!
HELLO, MOTHER. I WON'T STAY LONG, I PROMISE.
WHO IS YOUR HANDSOME LITTLE FRIEND?
THIS IS CECIL. HE'S A HUMAN. HE'S HAD... A FEW ACCIDENTS.
HI.
OH, I SEE. HIS PASSAGE HAS MADE HIM A BIT UNSTABLE. WELL, WE CAN HELP THAT A LITTLE...
THERE! MUCH BETTER!
MOM!
THIS IS THE MOST AWESOMEST DAY I'VE EVER HAD EVER!

BUT WHY RISK COMING HERE? THE POINT OF YOU LIVING ON EARTH WAS SO YOU COULD ESCAPE NOTICE BY THE LORDS OF ORDER AND CHAOS.
I... KIND OF MADE MYSELF KNOWN. I INVOKED A CHALLENGE.
OH. THAT'S... INTERESTING. AND THEY LET YOU GO?
YES. I ASSUME THAT MEANS I'M ALREADY INCLUDED IN THEIR PLANS.
PERHAPS. BUT YOU STILL HAVEN'T EXPLAINED WHY YOU'RE HERE.
I NEED TO MAKE MY WAY TO THE ROCK OF CHALLENGE. CECIL AND I BELIEVE AN INNOCENT PERSON IS BEING HELD PRISONER THERE.
AND THE PATH OF BEYOND WAS TOO TREACHEROUS, YES? VERY WELL. I CAN HELP YOU, BUT I WILL REQUIRE A BOON.
NAME IT.
NOT FROM YOU. FROM YOUR CECIL-FRIEND.
ME? WHAT CAN I DO?
FIRST, KNOW THAT WE OF CHAOS ARE NOT EVIL AS YOU KNOW IT; WE JUST HAVE... DIFFERENT VIEWS ON HOW TO DO THINGS THAN THOSE FROM THE HALLS OF ORDER.
OH... KAY?
THIS TALISMAN WILL GUIDE YOU TO THE ROCK OF CHALLENGE. PLACE IT ON THE GROUND THERE AND SAY [illegible]. IT WILL OPEN A GATEWAY BACK TO YOUR EARTH, ALLOWING YOU AND YOUR FRIENDS TO PASS SAFELY HOME.
BUT I CAN'T PRONOUNCE... UH...
OH RIGHT. HERE...
WHOA... DO I HAVE... TWO TONGUES NOW?
FOR THIS BARGAIN, YOU MUST PLACE THE TALISMAN ON THE GROUND AT THE STONE OF JUDGEMENT. DO NOT TAKE IT WITH YOU BACK TO EARTH.

MOTHER? WHAT ARE YOU PLANNING?
HUSH, MALPHAST. DO WE HAVE A BARGAIN?
WELL...
OF COURSE, LITTLE MORTAL! SO WE ARE AGREED?
SURE!
MOTHER, I DON'T WANT HIM TO HAVE REGRETS LATER.
YOU KNOW I HAVE TO OBEY CERTAIN RULES TO HELP, AND THE NEVERBORN MAKE THE DIRECT PATH TOO DANGEROUS...
WELL... YES, BUT...
THEN REST ASSURED THIS WILL NOT EVEN STAIN HIS SOUL ONE WHIT.
IT IS AN ACT THRICE REMOVED, AND BESIDES, IT WILL HOPEFULLY JUST MAKE THINGS MORE...
INTERESTING!
NOW HURRY ALONG! THE TALISMAN WILL GUIDE YOU SAFELY. I LOOK FORWARD TO MEETING MORE OF YOUR FRIENDS SOMEDAY!
THANK YOU, MOTHER.
I LOVE YOU!
I LOVE YOU, TOO.
YOUR MOM IS SO COOL! WHAT'S YOUR DAD LIKE?
THE WAY THIS DAY IS GOING, FRIEND CECIL, YOU'LL PROBABLY FIND OUT FOR YOURSELF.
THINK HE'LL GIVE ME, I DUNNO... MORE EYES?
I HOPE NOT...

LATER, BACK ON THE ROCK...
THAT WAS DEFINITELY NO SLUSHIE MACHINE. SO WHAT'S WITH THIS HELMET LOGO?
OH. THAT'S FOR SOME PLACE CALLED PRAETORIAN ACADEMY. CHARLES MUST GO TO SCHOOL THERE NOW.
WHAT KIND OF PLACE WOULD USE PROXIMITY SHOCK-COLLARS ON A STUDENT?
WELL... IT IS CHARLES WE'RE TALKING ABOUT.
GOOD POINT. HE MUST KNOW WHERE THEIR "SUPPLY CLOSET OF DOOM" IS.
WAIT... DO YOU HEAR THAT?
YEAH... BELLS?
HARPS?
THERE YOU GO, BOYS!
THANKS FOR THE RIDE, MR. MALPHAST'S DAD, SIR!
NOT AT ALL. NOW, FOR OUR BARGAIN...
I BEGIN TO UNDERSTAND WHY HUMAN CHILDREN DON'T LIKE THEIR PARENTS TRANSPORTING THEM IN FRONT OF THEIR FRIENDS.

DOES LETTING YOU MESS WITH THE PENDANT BREAK THE DEAL I MADE WITH MRS. MALPHAST?
NO, NO. WE DO THIS SORT OF THING **ALL** THE TIME; MOVE AND COUNTER-MOVE, SO GOES THE COSMIC BALANCE.
CECIL? WHAT... ARE YOU OKAY?
HEY. TYLER! YOU GOT HERE AHEAD OF ME. I GUESS THAT'S WHY THE BUREAU PUT YOU IN CHARGE.
AND MISS LANGDON. RIGHT? WE'RE HERE TO RESCUE YOU!
WAIT. CECIL HOLMES? MY MORNING CARBONATED CAFFEINE JUNKIE? ***THAT'S*** WHO YOU WERE TALKING ABOUT?
YEAH... BUT WITHOUT THE EARS, WINGS, AND... OTHER STUFF...
OH. THIS? MALPHAST'S DAD SAYS THIS'LL ALL CLEAR UP WHEN I GO BACK TO EARTH. I'LL ONLY LOOK LIKE THIS WHEN I GO HOPPING DIMENSIONS AND STUFF.
WHICH WE SHOULD DO OUR BEST TO ***PREVENT.***
THAT'S A RELIEF.
I DUNNO. I WAS REALLY GETTING TO LIKE THE CLAWS. BUT SMELLING THINGS WITH YOUR TUMMY IS **WEIRD.**
WITH YOUR ***WHAT?***
OKAY. EVERYONE GATHER AROUND. WE'RE GOING HOME.
THANK YOU, FATHER.
GLAD TO HELP. BE ***WELL***, SON. YOUR MOTHER AND I MISS YOU.

THE NEXT MOMENT, IN AN UNSUSPECTING SUBURB...
THANK GOODNESS WE'RE BACK IN... WHEREVER WE ARE.
WE ARE ON EARTH, RIGHT?
WE'RE IN MY FRONT YARD. I HOPE THE NEIGHBORS DIDN'T SEE ANYTHING; THEY DON'T HAVE THE CLEARANCE FOR THIS.
THANKS FOR SAVING US, GUYS. I NEVER THOUGHT I'D GET BACK.
IT WAS OUR PLEASURE, FRIEND TYLER. IT SEEMS TO HAVE ENDED WELL.

WE'LL PROBABLY GET IN TROUBLE FOR BEING ABSENT FROM SCHOOL.
I KNOW A GUY WHO KNOWS COMPUTERS. HE CAN PROBABLY FIX IT SO YOU DON'T GET NAILED FOR PLAYING HOOKY.
NOW I HAVE TO GET BACK TO MY STORE. STOP BY FOR SOME GOODIES ON THE HOUSE, OKAY?
THWARTING THOSE WHO THREATEN EARTH IS IT'S OWN REWARD... BUT I GUESS IT'D BE RUDE TO TURN DOWN FREE SODAS...
THEN I'LL SEE YOU TOMORROW FOR YOUR MORNING FILL-UP!
YES, GUYS, I MISSED YOU, TOO. WE'LL LINK UP ABOUT IT IN A FEW, OKAY?
THANKS FOR LETTING ME SEE... WELL, EVERYTHING, MALPHAST! I GUESS THERE'S MORE TO ALIEN BEINGS THAN OTHER PLANETS!
IT WAS A PLEASURE WORKING WITH YOU.
I'M JUST HAPPY IT'S OVER. WE'LL SEE YOU TOMORROW AT SCHOOL, OKAY CECIL?
YOU BET. WE'VE BOTH GOT REPORTS TO FILE WITH THE BUREAU TONIGHT.
OH, RIGHT. I ALMOST FORGOT... IN ALL THE EXCITEMENT.
FAREWELL, FRIEND CECIL.
BYE, GUYS!

OKAY, NOBODY'S WATCHING...
COMMENCE FIELD TEST NUMBER ONE!
HEEEYAAAAA!
I'M SO NEVER TAKING THIS COAT OFF AGAIN! NOT EVEN TO SHOWER!

BACK IN PS238...
YOU FOUND TYLER? YOU'RE SURE?
YES. I JUST CONFIRMED THE SIGHTING. HE AND SOME OTHER MISSING PERSONS JUST ARRIVED IN TOWN. DETAILS ARE SKETCHY AT THE MOMENT, BUT HE'S WELL.
THAT'S A RELIEF.
THEN YOU'VE GOT SOME SPACE IN YOUR SCHEDULE FOR THE NEXT CRISIS?
I PATCHED PROSPERO'S SCANNIN' GIZMO INTO OUR SYSTEM. SOMETHIN'S ON THE WAY, AND IT'S HUGE.
TRANSLATION MATRIX: Attempt 3444: Failed Attempt 3445: Failed Attempt 3446: Failed
INCOMING MASS COMPOSITION: UNKNOWN SILHOUETTE: UNKNOWN
WILL THE AUTHORITIES FINALLY TAKE THIS ALERT SERIOUSLY?
OH, HECK, YEAH. THEY AREN'T CLOAKIN' THEMSELVES OR ANYTHIN'. IT'S LIKE THEY WANNA BE SEEN. AND THAT'S NEVER A GOOD SIGN.
ROCKSLIDE SAYS IT USUALLY MEANS WE'RE MISSIN' SOMETHIN', OR THEY'RE SO STRONG THEY DON'T THINK WE CAN BEAT 'EM EVEN IF WE KNOW THEY'RE COMIN'.
IS IT GOING TO DROP ANY SURPRISES ON US?
I'M PRETTY SURE IT'S OUTTA OUR HANDS. WE GOT THE EARTH DEFENSE LEAGUE, THE POWER PARTNERS, AND JUST ABOUT EVERY HERO OUTFIT WITH SPACE TRAVEL CAPABILITY GETTIN' READY FOR IT.
THIS WAS THE KIND OF THING THAT WORRIED ME SICK WHEN I HELD ELECTED OFFICE...

"...NOBODY WANTS TO PRESIDE OVER AN INVASION."
TELL THE LORDS OF CHAOS THAT THE PENDANT DID ITS WORK. THE GATE IS STABLE. WE CAN REACH THE EARTH AGAIN, AND--
OH. "THEY" ARE HERE, TOO.
DO NOT CONFRONT THEM. THEY ARE IRRELEVANT TO OUR PURPOSES.
HEY, THIS IS JUST A SCOUTING MISSION. Y'KNOW, TO CHECK OUT THE REAL ESTATE.
ONCE AGAIN, OLD FOE, THERE ISN'T A PLACE YOU CAN INVADE THAT THE FORCES OF ORDER CAN'T FOLLOW YOU.
AND WHEN YOUR KIND COMES IN FORCE TO START TORMENTING THE HUMANS, WHAT WILL BE YOUR EXCUSE THEN?
THE USUAL. "THE DEVIL MADE ME DO IT."

"The earth? Oh the earth will be gone in a few seconds...I'm going to blow it up. It's obstructing my view of Venus."

- Marvin the Martian

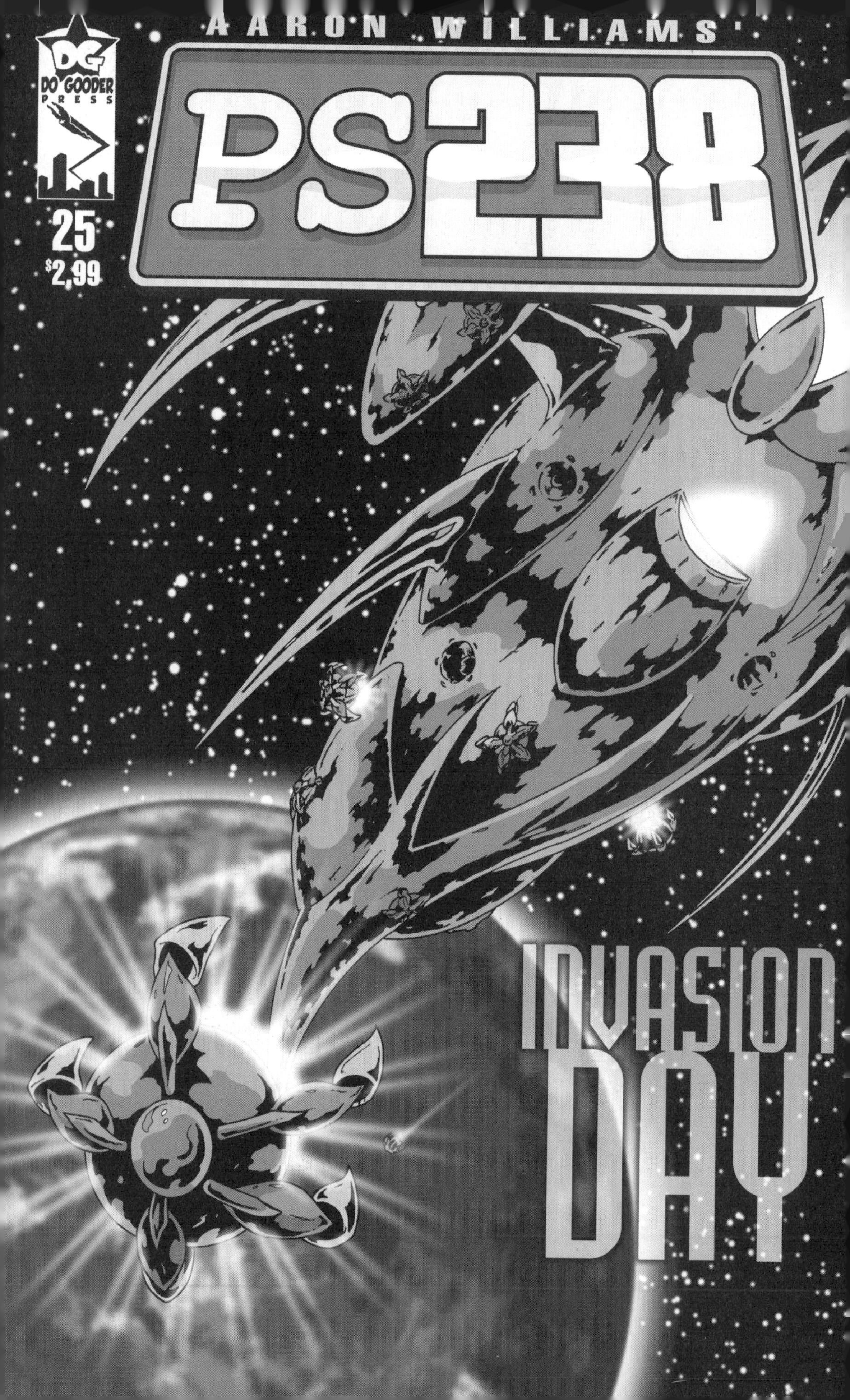
AARON WILLIAMS'
DO GOODER PRESS
PS238
25
$2,99
INVASION DAY

PS238
THE SCHOOL FOR METAPRODIGY CHILDREN
BY AARON WILLIAMS
FROM THE WAR JOURNAL OF CECIL HOLMES, BUREAU OF ALIEN MONITORING: IT'S HAPPENING. THE GOVERNMENT TRIED TO KEEP IT A SECRET, BUT WHEN THE EARTH DEFENSE LEAGUE, THE COSMOS LEGION AND A COUPLE OF OTHER SUPERHERO TEAMS WEREN'T ABLE TO STOP THE ALIEN WARSHIP, THE PRESIDENT WENT ON TV.
HE TOLD US THE ALIENS WERE COMING, AND NOBODY KNEW WHAT THEY WANTED WITH EARTH. THEY HADN'T BEEN HOSTILE TO THE ATTACKING HEROES; THE SHIP WAS JUST TOO BIG AND GOING TOO FAST FOR ANYONE TO STOP IT.
AT THE LAST MINUTE, EMERALD GAUNTLET AND ATLAS MANAGED TO DEFLECT THE SHIP ENOUGH THAT IT WOULDN'T CRASH INTO OUR PLANET...

I MEAN. SERIOUSLY. DIDN'T ANYBODY IN THE GOVERNMENT EVER SEE "WAR OF THE WORLDS?" IT'S NOT THE MOTHERSHIP YOU HAVE TO WATCH. WELL, UNLESS IT HOVERS OVER THE WHITE HOUSE AND STUFF.
THE ARMY HAS CLOSED UP THE BIG CITIES. OUR TOWN ISN'T CONSIDERED IMPORTANT ENOUGH FOR THAT, BUT THEY DON'T KNOW WHAT I KNOW. THEY'VE NEVER FACED AN ALIEN ON THEIR OWN PLAY-GROUND. AND I HAVE A HUNCH...
CITIZENS ARE ADVISED TO STAY INDOORS AND NOT GATHER IN LARGE GROUPS. THE INVASION CRAFT ARE EXPECTED TO ENTER THE ATMOSPHERE IN UNDER AN HOUR, THE WORLD'S AIRBORNE DEFENSES ARE BEING PREPARED...
THE INTERNET TO GO.
B·A·M
BUT IF THEY'RE MADE OF THE SAME MATERIAL AS THE MOTHERSHIP, IT'S EXPECTED THEY WILL HAVE TO BE DEALT WITH ON THE GROUND...
THEY'LL BE AT SCHOOL FOR PAYBACK. I LEFT MY FOLKS A NOTE LETTING THEM KNOW THE HOMEWORLD NEEDS ME, AND THAT I'LL TELL THEM WHAT I CAN WHEN I RETURN.
MEANWHILE, BENEATH CECIL'S SCHOOL AT PS238...
SHOULDN'T WE HAVE SENT THE CHILDREN HOME?
WE'RE THREE MILES UNDERGROUND. WHERE WOULD THEY BE SAFER?
TRY TELLING THEM THAT. A LOT OF THE KIDS WANT TO BE OUTSIDE TO HELP. KEVIN IS REALLY VOCAL ABOUT IT.
IS HE?
HIS DAD DID HELP GET RID OF THE MOTHERSHIP.
DO YOU HAVE ANY IDEA HOW MUCH TROUBLE WE'D GET IN IF WE EXPOSED OUR KIDS TO AN ALIEN INVASION?
MORE THAN I COULD DOCUMENT IN AN HOUR.

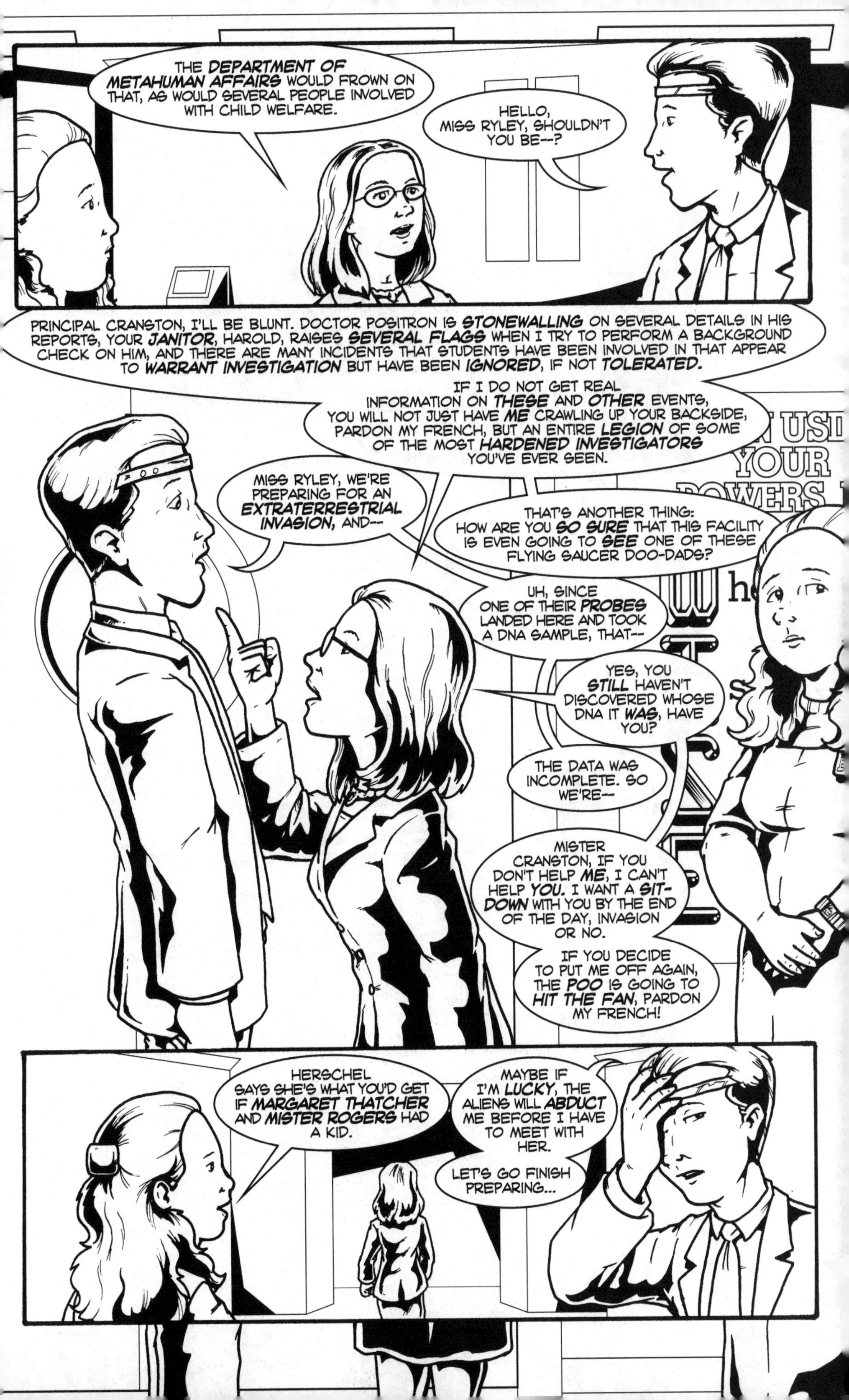
THE DEPARTMENT OF METAHUMAN AFFAIRS WOULD FROWN ON THAT, AS WOULD SEVERAL PEOPLE INVOLVED WITH CHILD WELFARE.
HELLO, MISS RYLEY, SHOULDN'T YOU BE--?
PRINCIPAL CRANSTON, I'LL BE BLUNT. DOCTOR POSITRON IS STONEWALLING ON SEVERAL DETAILS IN HIS REPORTS, YOUR JANITOR, HAROLD, RAISES SEVERAL FLAGS WHEN I TRY TO PERFORM A BACKGROUND CHECK ON HIM, AND THERE ARE MANY INCIDENTS THAT STUDENTS HAVE BEEN INVOLVED IN THAT APPEAR TO WARRANT INVESTIGATION BUT HAVE BEEN IGNORED, IF NOT TOLERATED.
IF I DO NOT GET REAL INFORMATION ON THESE AND OTHER EVENTS, YOU WILL NOT JUST HAVE ME CRAWLING UP YOUR BACKSIDE, PARDON MY FRENCH, BUT AN ENTIRE LEGION OF SOME OF THE MOST HARDENED INVESTIGATORS YOU'VE EVER SEEN.
YOUR
POWERS
MISS RYLEY, WE'RE PREPARING FOR AN EXTRATERRESTRIAL INVASION, AND--
THAT'S ANOTHER THING: HOW ARE YOU SO SURE THAT THIS FACILITY IS EVEN GOING TO SEE ONE OF THESE FLYING SAUCER DOO-DADS?
UH, SINCE ONE OF THEIR PROBES LANDED HERE AND TOOK A DNA SAMPLE, THAT--
YES, YOU STILL HAVEN'T DISCOVERED WHOSE DNA IT WAS, HAVE YOU?
THE DATA WAS INCOMPLETE. SO WE'RE--
MISTER CRANSTON, IF YOU DON'T HELP ME, I CAN'T HELP YOU. I WANT A SIT-DOWN WITH YOU BY THE END OF THE DAY, INVASION OR NO.
IF YOU DECIDE TO PUT ME OFF AGAIN, THE POO IS GOING TO HIT THE FAN, PARDON MY FRENCH!
HERSCHEL SAYS SHE'S WHAT YOU'D GET IF MARGARET THATCHER AND MISTER ROGERS HAD A KID.
MAYBE IF I'M LUCKY, THE ALIENS WILL ABDUCT ME BEFORE I HAVE TO MEET WITH HER.
LET'S GO FINISH PREPARING...

CECIL'S WAR DIARY. I HAD TO DODGE THE POLICE PATROLS. I DIDN'T NEED TO EXPLAIN TO THEM YET AGAIN THAT THEY'RE INTERFERING WITH GOVERNMENT BUSINESS EVERY TIME THEY STOP ME AND TAKE ME HOME. I WEAR MY "PUBLIC NUISANCE" CITATIONS WITH HONOR... ALTHOUGH THE DIRECTOR THINKS OTHERWISE.
SPEAKING OF WHOM...
AGENT HOLMES, YOU DIDN'T LEAVE YOUR HOUSE, DID YOU?
CAN YOU ASSUME I TOLD YOU "NO," YOU DIDN'T BELIEVE ME, AND THEN I PROMISED I'D GO BACK, BUT DIDN'T?
I SUPPOSE I'LL *HAVE* TO...
WE'RE TRACKING SEVERAL OF THESE INBOUND CRAFT. THEY BYPASSED A NUMBER OF ORBITAL DEFENSE PLATFORMS WITHOUT A *SCRATCH*, WHICH IS A BIT DISAPPOINTING GIVEN HOW MUCH I *PAID* FOR THEM.
SO *PLEASE* DON'T DO ANYTHING THAT MIGHT GET YOU *ZAPPED*. IF YOU *MUST* BE OUT, TRY TO ESCORT OTHERS TO SAFETY AND PROTECT THEM AS BEST YOU CAN. HOW'S THAT?
OH, SURE. I'LL BE ON THE LOOKOUT FOR SURVIVORS.
I'M SURE YOU WILL.
SIGH...
REPORT IN IF YOU SEE ANY ALIEN ACTIVITY, AT LEAST. I MIGHT BE ABLE TO SEND SOME HELP YOUR WAY.
ROGER AND OUT!
I DO LIKE THE DIRECTOR, BUT HE'S SO *OVER-PROTECTIVE*. YOU'D THINK I HADN'T BEEN AT THIS JOB FOR MY *ENTIRE LIFE* OR SOMETHING...
MAYBE WHEN WE FINALLY MEET IN PERSON, HE'LL SEE I'M MORE THAN--
UH-OH. TIME TO GO TO *WORK*...

MEANWHILE, IN PS238'S DORMITORIES...
LOCK OVERRIDE ACCEPTED. THANK YOU FOR HACKING CLAY INDUSTRIES' UNBREAKABLE ALGORITHM.
...AND IF HE SHOWS UP, TRY TO KEEP HIM OUT OF TROUBLE.
WHY ME? WHY NOT CALL THE TEACHERS TO GET CECIL?
THEY'LL PROBABLY BE TOO BUSY, AND HE THINKS THEY'RE ALIENS, TOO; HE MIGHT START USING HIS SHRINK RAY ON FRIEND AND FOE ALIKE.
OH. OKAY. BUT WHAT ABOUT THE REAL ALIENS?
THEY DON'T SEEM TO BE INTERESTED IN MILITARY CONQUEST THUS FAR.
I'M NOT SURE WHAT THEY WANT, BUT THEY DON'T SEEM TO BE MAKING A GREAT EFFORT TO HURT THE POPULATION.
THEY HURT ME A LITTLE LAST TIME. THEY POKED MY CHEEK WITH THAT NEEDLE-THING.
WHAT NEEDLE-THING?
BEFORE I USED MY GRAPPLER MAGNET TO MAKE THEIR PROBE-THING GO ALL FUNNY, THIS NEEDLE POKED ME IN THE FACE. IT KIND OF STUNG.
I SEE...
I THINK WE'RE BEING DISTRACTED FROM THE REAL THREAT, HERE. TYLER, WHATEVER YOU DO DON'T--
BZZRT!
--GO OUTSIDE.
TYLER? DO YOU COPY?
* PS238 #22
PROCEEDING TO GROUND LEVEL. THANK YOU FOR USING CLAY INDUSTRIES' LOCKERVATOR.
REVENANT? HELLO?
AT THAT SAME MOMENT...
I LOST MY CONNECTION TO WASHINGTON. WHAT'S GOING ON?
THE THING PUT OUT AN EM PULSE OR SOMETHIN'. OUR SYSTEMS ARE OKAY, BUT CELL PHONES, RADIOS, THE WHOLE SHEBANG IS OUT FOR A WHILE.
I THINK THAT'S OUR CUE. LET'S GO STOMP SOME ALIENS.

BACK FOR MORE, HUH?
I BROUGHT MY SHRINK RAY AND PLENTY OF OLIVE JARS, SO BRING IT ON!
CECIL!
CECIL, LET'S GO! REV-- UH, YOUR BOSS CALLED ME AND SAID TO GET YOU INSIDE!
TYLER, WHAT ARE YOU DOING WEARING... THAT?
YOU RECOGNIZED ME?
DUH. WHO COULDN'T TELL IT WAS YOU?
I USED TO THINK THAT, TOO, BUT--
BZORT!
BZORT!
BZORT!
BZORT!

COOL. ARE THOSE ELECTRO-MAGNETS?
PROBABLY.
YOU!
YOU'RE THE ONE! YOU AND MISS KYLE!
HUH?
GET LOST, ZODON. WE'VE GOT OTHER ALIENS TO THWART TODAY.
THAT'S EXACTLY WHY I'M HERE. SOMEBODY HAS TO GET RELIABLE INTEL FROM THE BATTLEFIELD, AND I DON'T TRUST THOSE LAWN SPRINKLERS RUNNING THIS SCHOOL TO DELIVER.
AS MUCH AS IT GALLS ME, I'M PROBABLY GOING TO WIND UP SAVING EVERYBODY'S KNOCK-WURSTS FROM THESE INTERGALACTIC TULIP BULBS.
THESE FLYING THINGS ARE JUST ROBOTS, AREN'T THEY? LET'S GET THE REAL ALIENS! C'MON!
IT'S A FREE-FOR-ALL, PEOPLE!
TAKE OUT AS MANY AS YOU CAN AND CLOSE ON THE SPACESHIP!
CRISTI, YOU'RE WITH ME! I'M GONNA TOSS YOU ON TOP OF THAT THING WHILE I TRY TO KEEP IT OCCUPIED FROM BELOW.
THEN WE CLEAR OUT FOR HERSCHEL'S "WEATHER FORECAST."

I WISH I HADN'T DRESSED IN SUCH A HURRY TODAY; I'M GOING TO LOOK SILLY FIGHTING ALIENS IN MY DENIM DRESS.
IT SHOULD SERVE. IT'S MADE OF UNSTABLE MOLE-CULES, YES?
YOU BET. NOTHING FIGHTS STAINS FROM KIDS ARMED WITH FINGER PAINT BETTER. MY WHOLE WARDROBE IS MADE FROM THE STUFF.
IF I EVER RETIRE. I'M MAKING MY OWN LINE OF CLOTHES FOR TEACHERS.
IT'S GOOD TO HAVE PLANS FOR THE FUTURE, ASSUMING WE WIN TODAY.
THIS THING IS FILLED WITH NOTHING BUT FLYING--
HEY! WHAT ARE THOSE KIDS DOING OUT HERE?!
KIDS? WHERE?
THERE'S THREE HALF-PINTS UP HERE HEADED FOR THE SPACESHIP! AND...
THEY'RE ACTUALLY DOING PRETTY WELL AGAINST THESE FLYING GIZMOS.
WHAT KIND OF VISUAL DO YOU HAVE ON THEM? WHO ARE THEY?
I CAN'T TRIGGER THE SATELLITES IF THERE ARE KIDS TOPSIDE! THEY'LL GET KILLED!
STAND BY.
PRINCIPAL CRANSTON!
WHAT IS IT, UH... POSITRON NUMBER TWO? WE'VE KIND OF GOT A SITUATION...
WE FINISHED ANALYZING THE DNA DATA FROM THE PROBE. I THINK WE KNOW WHO IT GOT A SAMPLE OF. HERE.

TYLER MARLOCKE? THEY GOT HIS DNA?
I GOT A GLIMPSE OF THE KIDS. ONE'S A BUZZ-CUT IN AN OVERCOAT WITH WHAT LOOKS LIKE A SHRINK GUN, I THINK THE SECOND ONE IS ZODON...
AND THE OTHER ONE IS IN A BLACK CAPE THROWING GADGETS AND OTHER TECH STUFF AT THESE THINGS. ANY IDEA WHO THAT IS?
THE ONE WITH THE COAT IS PROBABLY CECIL HOLMES. THE OTHER ONE SOUNDS LIKE A CHILD VERSION OF...
2 + 2 = R
OH... NO...
TYLER ISN'T IN HIS DORM ROOM, IS HE?
ER, NO, I CHECKED ON THE WAY OVER HERE AND--
SOMEONE GET THOSE CHILDREN OUT OF THERE. LET US KNOW WHEN THEY'RE OUT OF HARM'S WAY.
GET THAT CONDUCTOR IN PLACE AFTER YOU'RE DONE. IF THAT SHIP GETS OUT OF RANGE...
ROGER THAT.
CRISTI?
MY MOLECULES ARE AS DENSE AS I CAN MAKE THEM.
SAVE THE TYKES AND THEN WE'LL TRY TO SALVAGE THE PLAN.

WE'RE ALMOST THERE!
GOOD, BECAUSE I'M OUT OF THESE DISC THINGS. ZODON, WHY AREN'T YOU HELPING?
I'M JUST USING MY HOLO-PROJECTOR, A MINIATURE ANTI-GRAV DRONE, AND A REMOTE SENSOR ARRAY. YOU DON'T THINK A SUPER GENIUS IS DUMB ENOUGH TO BE OUT IN THE MIDDLE OF A FIREFIGHT, DO YOU?
OKAY, BOYS, RECESS IS OVER. TIME TO GO INSIDE.
I'M OWED ALL APOLOGY FROM YOU, BLONDIE! YOU AND COMMANDER FOOTBALL, HERE SHOVED ME--
WE DON'T HAVE TIME FOR THIS! YOU THREE ARE IN THE WAY OF--
WAIT, "BLONDIE?!"
AS THE ONLY DULY APPOINTED FEDERAL AGENT HERE, I'D LIKE TO--
LOOK OUT!
OH, NEVER MIND. IT'S NOT WORTH CAUSING A TEMPORAL PARADOX.
I'LL LECTURE YOU TWO LATER.

I CAN'T GET FREE! CAN YOU DO ANYTHING?
I CAN MESS THEM UP WITH MY GRAPPLER MAGNET...
...BUT I GOTTA HELP CECIL FIRST!
...AND IF YOU CEASE ALL HOSTILITIES, I'LL MAKE SURE YOU'RE STUDIED HUMANELY.
CHUNK!
WE'LL NEVER GIVE UP AND NEVER SURRENDER!
EARTH FOR THE WIN! EARTH FOR THE WIN!!!
GOOD JOB, COAT.
NOW... LET'S SEE IF WE CAN'T BREAK INTO THIS THING.

MEANWHILE, ONBOARD THE ALIEN SHIP...
SO... WHY DID IT DROP US IN HERE?
I DON'T KNOW. PROBABLY BECAUSE WE'RE NOT CONSIDERED A THREAT.
OH. WHAT DO WE--
MOON SHADOW? ARE YOU THERE? COME IN.
I'M HERE!
WHAT?
I'VE GOT A HELMET-PHONE THING AND I'M GETTING A CALL.
THE INTER-FERENCE FINALLY CLEARED UP AND I'M ALMOST TO YOUR POSITION. WHATEVER YOU DO, DON'T GO OUTSIDE OR GO NEAR THE SPACE-SHIP.
WELL... I'M KIND OF ALREADY ON THE SHIP.
OH. THAT'S DISAPPOINTING...
YOU'RE TELLING ME.
...BECAUSE I THINK YOU MIGHT BE KEY TO THE ALIENS' PLANS.
HOW?
MISS KYLE? GLAD TO SPEAK WITH YOU AGAIN. I THINK YOU CALLED YOURSELF "MICRO MIGHT" THE LAST TIME WE SPOKE, BUT THAT WAS SOME TIME AGO.
WHO--?
I THINK I KNOW SOMEONE WHO CAN HELP DEFEAT THE INVADERS, BUT I NEED SOME TIME. DO YOU THINK YOU CAN FIND A WAY OUT OF THE SHIP?
I DON'T KNOW. THEY DUMPED US IN A LAUNCH BAY, AND SO FAR, I HAVEN'T HAD MUCH LUCK EVEN DENTING THE HULL.
PLEASE TRY. THE PLANET MIGHT DEPEND ON IT.

OH, GOOD. NO PRESSURE, THEN.
WHO'S TALKIN' TO CRISTI?
THE REVENANT.
ON AN OPEN CHANNEL?
HE'S LETTING US KNOW THE SITUATION.
AND THAT SITUATION WOULD BE COMPLETELY CARWASHED.
I COULD'VE THOUGHT UP EIGHT WAYS TO ATOMIZE THE INVADERS AND COMPLETED SIX OF THEM BY NOW!
THIS IS A COMMAND CENTER? IT NEEDS MORE OPEN FLAMES.
WHAT ARE YOU TWO DOING HERE?
ENSURING THE SURVIVAL OF THE PLANET. WE COULDN'T LEAVE A FIGHT FOR EARTH TO THE LIKES OF YOU.
I DON'T SUPPOSE YOU'VE PICKED UP ON THE TRANSMISSIONS FROM THE JUPITER TWO OUT THERE, HAVE YOU?
HERSCHEL?
WHAT? AW, HECK! THEY'RE ON TV!
--HAVE BRED A DISEASE. OUR VECTOR IS CAPTURED. INFECTED, MUTATION WILL COMMENCE. SPREADING DISEASE OVER YOUR WORLD. DISEASE NOT FATAL. DISEASE CHANGES GENOME.
ALL FUTURE HUMAN GENERATIONS BECOME LIKE US. YOU ARE FUTURE OF US. YOUR BREEDING ARE BECOME OUR CHILDREN. YOU CANNOT PREVAIL. EMBRACE THIS NOW AND FOR ALL FUTURE.

VECTOR? THEY'VE GOT A BIO-WEAPON?
IT SHOULD BE OBVIOUS. THEY'VE GOT SOMEONE ON BOARD ONE OF THEIR SHIPS THAT'S GOING TO BE A TYPHOID MARY, SPREADING AN ENGINEERED DISEASE ACROSS THE GLOBE.
IT'S GOING TO ALTER OUR DNA SO ANY FUTURE GENERATIONS OF HUMANS WILL LOOK LIKE THOSE WALKING SEAFOOD PLATTERS. THEY'RE GOING TO USE HUMANITY TO PERPETUATE THEIR SPECIES.
WE HAVE GOT TO GET THEM OUT--
WHAT THE--? DID ONE OF YOU TWO OVERRIDE MY LOCKDOWN ON THE SCHOOL ELEVATORS?!
NO.
NOT THAT WE COULDN'T HAVE HAD WE WANTED TO.
PS238 SECURITY ISN'T EVEN UP TO "CHEESEBALL" STANDARDS.
LOCKER-VATOR TWELVE WAS ALREADY OPEN.
AND IT WASN'T LIKE--
STOP TOUCHIN' STUFF!
PRINCIPAL CRANSTON? POSITRON HERE...
I DON'T KNOW IF YOU CAN SEE THIS, BUT THE SHIP IS MOBILE AND HAS OUR TEAM DOWN.
STILL NO SIGN OF MISS KYLE. THE ENERGY OUTPUT OF THE FLYING DRONES' WEAPONS HAS INCREASED IN LETHALITY.
DAMAGE TO MY SYSTEMS MAY FORCE ME TO SHUT DOWN AND GIVE MY SELF-REPAIR A CHANCE TO STABILIZE THINGS, BUT--
I HOPE TO-- OH...
HI. I FIX STUFF. YOU LOOKED LIKE YOU COULD USE IT.
THANK YOU, KATHARINE. BUT IT'S DANGEROUS OUT HERE!
I KNOW. THAT'S WHY THEY CAME OUT, TOO!

I GUESS WE BLAST IT, HUH?
THAT WOULD BE MY STRATEGY FOR THE MOMENT.
YOU'RE SURE I WON'T GET IN TROUBLE? I USUALLY GET FROWNY-FACES AT ME WHEN I GO NUCULER.
BERNARD BREAK STUFF!
LOOK ON THE BRIGHT SIDE, SUZI; IF YOU GET FROWNY-FACES, IT MEANS EVERYONE IS STILL ALIVE.
HEAVIER... THAN... IT LOOKS...
ARE YOU OKAY, COACH?
THEY TALKED ME INTO IT.
WHAT'RE YOU DOING OUT HERE?

YOU'RE A HEALER, AND PEOPLE OUT HERE ARE GONNA NEED HEALING. AND SINCE YOU BROUGHT ME BACK FROM THE DEAD, I'LL BET MY GUARDIAN IS GOING TO KEEP YOU NICE AND SAFE, TOO.
NOW, IT LOOKS LIKE MISS VASHTI'S GOT AN OWIE.
AND GUARDIAN? YOU BETTER KEEP VERN SAFE, OR I WON'T TALK TO YOU FOR A MONTH!
I CAN'T BELIEVE YOU TALKED ME INTO THIS!
MEANWHILE, IN THE SPACESHIP...
YOU SHOULD HAVE TRIED TO GET AWAY, LIKE I TOLD YOU TO.
I COULDN'T JUST LET THEM GRAB YOU! SO... CAN YOU SHRINK OUT OF THESE CUFF-THINGS?
I TRIED. THEY ADJUST.
CAN YOU CALL FOR HELP?
THE CUFFS SMASHED MY RADIO-WATCH.
HUMAN AIR-TALK STOPS.
GENETIC-PATTERN HUMAN, BECOME YOU VESSEL FOR OUR GENERATIONS.
GO. MUTATE. MAKE ALL HUMANS TO BE VESSELS. MANY YOUNGLINGS OF OUR KIND.
WE WERE FINALITY OF RACE. YOU ARE BEGINNING. GREAT HONOR.
WHAT? IS HE SAYING I'M GOING TO HAVE BABIES? I DON'T WANT THAT!
WHATEVER HAPPENS, MOON SHADOW, WE'LL--
EAT DAT! AND DAT! GO BACK T' RED LOBSTA AND HOP ONNA BUFFET!
BOOM! BANG! WHAMM!

DAT'S RIGHT! ANGIE AND P-DUDE GONNA KICK WHATEVER YOU SITS ON!
PROSP-O'S SPACE-TECH GUNK DID THE TRICK: YOU GOT'CHER HOLES, REV-DUDE! GO GET 'EM!
BOO
THANK YOU, ANGIE. AND YOU, TOO. PROSPERO.
I'LL ASSUME THAT MEANT "GOOD LUCK."
I THINK ONE OF US IS GOING TO NEED A BIGGER GUN, MY TENTACLED FR--

THANKS FOR DISTRACTING IT, CITIZEN.
I'M STILL NOT USED TO MY WINGS, AND IT'S HARD TO GET A STEADY SHOT.
AH... IS IT?
I'M AGENT HOLMES WITH THE BUREAU OF ALIEN MONITORING. I'M OFFICIALLY DEPUTIZING YOU TO HELP ME NEUTRALIZE THIS THREAT.
NOW FOLLOW ME AND TRY NOT TO GET IN THE WAY.
BINK!
OH... KAY?
YOU COMING OR NOT?
SORRY. IT'S BEEN A WEIRD KIND OF DAY.
YOU'LL GET USED TO IT. IT TOOK ME A FEW MINUTES, TOO.
BY THE WAY, HOW MANY OTHER ALIEN RACES ARE WE WORKING WITH, HERE? I'LL HAVE TO CALL MY DIRECTOR AND REQUEST TO BE BETTER INFORMED...

KEEP AWAY FROM HIM!
YOU HEARD THE LADY.
THEY DIDN'T GET YOU WITH THAT NEEDLE, DID THEY, MOON SHADOW?
NO, I'M FINE, THANKS!
GOOD. LET'S GET EVERYONE OUT OF HERE SO--
AHEM. I'M THE ONE IN CHARGE HERE, YOU KNOW. FEDERAL JURISDICTION.
YOU'RE--
LET'S GET OUT OF HERE BEFORE MORE OF THE SHIP'S CREW SHOWS UP.
MY DEPUTY HERE CAME IN A PLANE WHICH I HOPE TO USE FOR OUR ESCAPE. FAILING THAT, I'LL FLY YOU ALL TO THE GROUND ONE AT A TIME.
OH, NO...

WHAT? IT'S NOT LIKE I CAN'T GLIDE, EVEN WITH THE ADULTS, PROBABLY.
I THINK I'M REALLY IN TROUBLE...
QUARRANTINE. WHERE'S THE NEAREST QUARANTINE AREA? IS THERE ONE ON YOUR CAMPUS?
I-I THINK SO, BUT WE'VE NEVER HAD TO--
GET HIM THERE AS SOON AS POSSIBLE! THERE'S A HOLE IN THE HULL BACK DOWN THE CORRIDOR. USE IT TO ESCAPE BEFORE IT'S TOO LATE. HURRY!
THEY'VE GIVEN HIM A VIRUS BASED ON HIS DNA. WHEN IT MUTATES, IT'LL INFECT THE REST OF THE PLANET.
YOU'VE GOT TO GO NOW!
ALL RIGHT, BUT... I'LL TRY TO SEND HELP!
THIS ONE'S GOT BATTLE ARMOR. WE'LL SEE IF IT LOOKS GOOD IN A SIZE "SMALL!"

YOU SHOULD HAVE RUN! NEXT TIME, WHEN A GROWN-UP TELLS YOU TO RUN, YOU RUN!
I GUESS IT'S TOO LATE TO SAY I'M SORRY, ISN'T IT?
CLASS DISMISSED!
PS238

"War is much too serious to be left to military men."

- *Charles-Maurice de Talleyrand-Perigord*

AARON WILLIAMS'
PS238
DG DO GOODER PRESS
26
$2.99
QUARANTINE

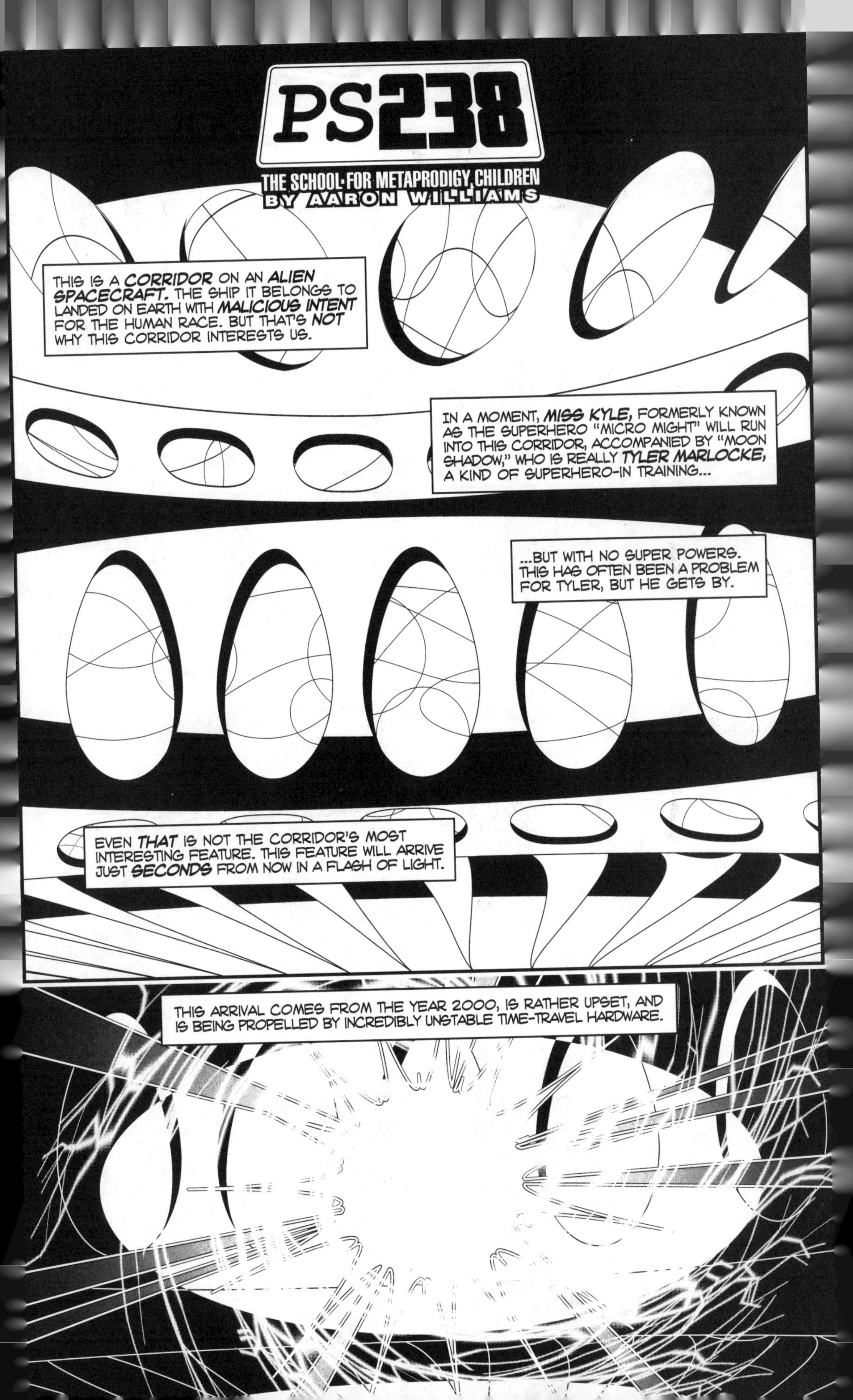
PS238
THE SCHOOL FOR METAPRODIGY CHILDREN
BY AARON WILLIAMS
THIS IS A CORRIDOR ON AN ALIEN SPACECRAFT. THE SHIP IT BELONGS TO LANDED ON EARTH WITH MALICIOUS INTENT FOR THE HUMAN RACE. BUT THAT'S NOT WHY THIS CORRIDOR INTERESTS US.
IN A MOMENT, MISS KYLE, FORMERLY KNOWN AS THE SUPERHERO "MICRO MIGHT" WILL RUN INTO THIS CORRIDOR, ACCOMPANIED BY "MOON SHADOW," WHO IS REALLY TYLER MARLOCKE, A KIND OF SUPERHERO-IN TRAINING...
...BUT WITH NO SUPER POWERS. THIS HAS OFTEN BEEN A PROBLEM FOR TYLER, BUT HE GETS BY.
EVEN THAT IS NOT THE CORRIDOR'S MOST INTERESTING FEATURE. THIS FEATURE WILL ARRIVE JUST SECONDS FROM NOW IN A FLASH OF LIGHT.
THIS ARRIVAL COMES FROM THE YEAR 2000, IS RATHER UPSET, AND IS BEING PROPELLED BY INCREDIBLY UNSTABLE TIME-TRAVEL HARDWARE.

MY COORDINATES SAY THIS SHOULD BE THE EXCELSIOR SCHOOLYARD... BUT...
DID I SWITCH GOLFING PLANETS OR SOMETHING?
BZORRT!
WHAT THE HATCHBACK--?
CURRENT APR: 549%

POP!
HOW DID YOU GET IN HERE?! YOU'RE SUPPOSED TO BE OUTSIDE!
OUTSIDE? AND WHERE'S TYLER? MY DAY JUST GOT WORSE SO HE'S GOT TO BE CLOSE BY!
PLEASE TELL ME THAT THING OVER THERE ATE HIM.
WAIT... MISS KYLE! HE YELLED AT YOU ABOUT THIS BEFORE!
YELLED? OH.
BUT IT GOES...
SO WE SHOULD...
WE NEED IT GONE.
YOU'RE RIGHT.
HEY!
WHAT THE HULA HOOP ARE YOU DOING?!

THIS IS CHILD ENDANGERMENT! I'LL SEE THE BOTH OF YOU--
--IN COURT! YOU'LL HEAR FROM MY LAWYER...
DEET-DEET-DEET-DEET-DEET-DEET-DEET...
SO HOW DID HE KNOW TO YELL AT US EARLIER FOR DOING SOMETHING WE HADN'T DONE YET?
AND SINCE WHEN COULD HE DISAPPEAR LIKE THAT?
HE WAS TRAVELING THROUGH TIME. BUT DON'T WORRY, TOM TELLS ME HE WON'T TRY IT AGAIN.
HE TOLD YOU?
AREN'T WE SUPPOSED TO BE GOING TO QUARTER-TEEN?
QUARANTINE! CRUD! WE'VE GOTTA GO!

IS IT JUST ME, OR IS THIS THING BIGGER ON THE INSIDE THAN IT IS ON THE OUTSIDE?
WAIT! I HEAR VOICES!
I DON'T SUPPOSE YOU'LL LISTEN IF I TELL YOU TO RUN, WILL YOU?
YOU MEAN BACK TOWARDS THE ALIENS?
NEVER MIND.
UGH, ROCKSLIDE WAS ALWAYS BETTER AT THIS STRATEGY STUFF THAN ME.
PLEASE DON'T BE SOMETHING THAT LOOKS LIKE A GIANT COCKROACH...

KEVIN?!
UH... HI, MISS KYLE.
BUS-TED.
WE SHOULDN'A GONE OUTSIDE, SHOULD WE?
NO SMASH?
I WILL NOT RETREAT. MY MOTOR-CYCLE MUST BE AVENGED!
MORE TAXPAYER MONEY WASTED...
SO... ARE WE IN, LIKE... LOTSA TROUBLE?
ABOUT AS MUCH AS THE SCHOOL IS, NOW...
COME IN, MOON SHADOW.
HELLO? REVENANT? DID YOU BEAT THE ALIENS?
THE ONES IN ARMOR ARE PROVING RESISTANT TO MOST ATTACKS, BUT MORE IMPORTANTLY: HAVE YOU MADE IT SAFELY OUTSIDE YET?
NOT REALLY. WE KINDA RAN INTO... STUFF.
CAN YOU PASS YOUR HEADSET TO MISS KYLE?
SURE. HANG ON.
IT'S FOR YOU.
NOW?
IT'S THE REVENANT.

HEY! IT'S MOON SHADOW! WE CAN'T LOSE NOW!
YES? I KNOW.
WE RAN INTO ONE OF THOSE ALIEN MONSTERS!
I DO REALIZE THE FATE OF THE PLANET IS AT STAKE AND...
YES. I. KNOW!
MOON SHADOW CAN'T STAY AND...
...I CAN'T BELIEVE I'M SAYING THIS...
...HELP STOP THE ALIENS. WE HAVE--
WAIT. DON'T TELL THEM ABOUT THE VIRUS. TELL THEM YOU'RE LEAVING FOR A DIFFERENT REASON.
WAIT, WHAT? WE'RE LEAVING BECAUSE..?
I AM NOT SAYING THAT.
YES, HE IS ADMIRED, BUT--
FINE...
I'VE BEEN... INJURED AND MOON SHADOW HAS TO... ESCORT ME TO SAFETY.
WE'LL FIGHT IN HIS NAME!
PLEASE DON'T DO ANYTHING THAT'LL GET THE SCHOOL IN EVEN MORE TROUBLE...
SO WHERE'S EITHER THE CONTROL ROOM OR THE FRONT LINE IN THIS CONFLICT?
THAT WAY. LOOK FOR A MAN WITH A BLACK CAPE. HE'S CALLED THE REVENANT.

OR AS I'M CALLING HIM, "CAPTAIN IN LOCO PARENTIS." HE'S...
..HE'S MOON SHADOW'S SIDEKICK.
I DIDN'T QUITE COPY THAT.
HE'S ALSO A LITTLE GRUMPY, BUT DO YOUR BEST TO WORK WITH HIM.
WE'VE STOOD AROUND LONG ENOUGH! LET'S--
K-THOOOOOMMMM
ANGIE'S JUNK-BOT MUST'VE COME BACK FOR ROUND TWO.
FOR MOON SHADOW!
FOR FREEDOM!
SMASHY-TIME! SMASHY-TIME!
YOU DON'T HAVE YOUR OWN P.R. DEPARTMENT IN THAT UTILITY BELT, DO YOU?
I DON'T THINK SO. WHAT'S A--?
SKIP IT. I THINK I SEE DAYLIGHT...

YOU CHUMPS BE PAYIN' FOR WRECKIN' MY RIDE!
OHHHH... CRUD.
WHAT'S HAPPENING? WHY ARE ARE THERE MORE OF THESE SPACESHIP THINGS?!
I THINK YOUR FAN CLUB JUST GOT A BUNCH OF NEW MEMBERS.
I HOPE SOMEONE FROM MY TEAM IS AROUND...
I SEE THEM! DO YOU HAVE A FLARE GUN OR SOMETHING WE COULD USE TO GET THEIR ATTENTION?
I THINK SO...
MISS KYLE SPOTTED DR. POSITRON AND SPELL SYRIN, WHO HAVE THEIR HANDS FULL...
I'M STILL HAVING PROBLEMS WITH MAKING THESE BEINGS PERCIEVE MY ILLUSIONS, AND HAVING TO RESORT TO SHIELDING AND OFFENSIVE SPELLS IS QUITE TAXING.
I'M MORE CONCERNED ABOUT THE NEW ARRIVALS. UNLESS WE CAN FORMULATE SOME SORT OF PLAN TO TAKE OUT THESE CRAFT, WE'RE--
WHAT IS THAT?

HLEP
HEPL
EITHER THE ALIENS LEARNED HOW TO SPELL FROM THE INTERNET...
I'M ZOOMING IN ON THE SHIP...
IT'S MISS KYLE! LET'S GO!
DON'T WORRY, I'VE GOT ANOTHER SIGNAL. THESE GLOVES MAKE TYPING ON THIS LITTLE LETTER PAD THING HARD, AND I'M SORTA NERVOUS.
I HAVE SOME OTHER STUFF I'VE NEVER USED, BUT IT'S ALL MARKED WITH ORANGE "WARNING" STICKERS, SO--
IT WORKED!
ARE ALL OF THESE SPACECRAFT HERE FOR YOU TWO?
PROBABLY. THEY GAVE MOON SHADOW A VIRUS. IT'S GOING TO MUTATE AND SPREAD IF WE DON'T GET HIM BACK TO PS238!
DID YOU GET THAT, PRINCIPAL CRANSTON?

WE DID. GET HIM BACK HERE AS SOON AS POSSIBLE. WE HAVE A STASIS UNIT SET UP IN LAB FOUR. YOU CAN MEET US THERE.
WE'VE RECONFIGURED YOUR "LIGHTING ROD" PLAN TO BE ABOUT TWENTY TIMES MORE KICK-DOILY THAN IT WAS...
BUT YOUR RELIANCE ON AN IONIZING DEVICE TO TRIGGER IT INCREASES THE POSSIBILITY OF FAILURE BEYOND MEASURE.
I DON'T SUPPOSE YOU'VE GOT A POLARIZATION EMITTER SOMEWHERE? IF NOT, WE'LL HAVE TO MAKE ONE FROM THE HUMMUS YOU CALL A COMPUTER NETWORK.
MEANWHILE, ABOVEGROUND, NEAR THE FLAGPOLE...
SATORI! WHAT ARE YOU DOING HERE? THE SKY MACHINES MIGHT FIND AND HURT YOU!
I DIDN'T WANT TO COME, BUT THE BLUE LADY CAME TO ME AGAIN.
SHE'S THE ONE WHO TOLD ME HOW TO MAKE MY PARENTS MOVE HERE IN THE FIRST PLACE.
THIS "BLUE LADY." SHE IS A SPIRIT, LIKE I AM?
UH-HUH. AND SHE TOLD ME TO FIND YOU.
WHY?
THAT TO HELP STOP THE ALIENS, I HAVE TO LET YOU POSSESS ME.
HOW WOULD THAT DO ANY GOOD FOR ANYONE?
SHE DIDN'T SAY, JUST THAT I WAS THE ONLY ONE WHO COULD BE A... A HOST.
AND THAT I HAVE TO TAKE THE CHANCE THAT... THOSE THINGS I WORRY ABOUT FINDING ME...
...THAT THEY DON'T NOTICE US. WHEN I LET GHOSTS USE ME, THAT'S HOW IT FOUND ME BEFORE.
C'MON, BEFORE ONE OF THOSE SPACEMAN-THINGS SHOWS UP.
VERY WELL... IF YOU SAY WE SHOULD...
OH... I SEE... AND I CAN...
SATORI, I THINK WE CAN HELP.

YOU "CAN HELP?" WHO IS THIS, AND HOW DID YOU GET ON THIS CHANNEL?
I... DON'T KNOW MY NAME. BUT I AM WITH THE SATORI CHILD.
AIN'T SHE THE ONE WHO SEES GHOSTS AN' STUFF?
I LIVED HERE MANY YEARS AGO. YOU CALL MY PEOPLE "NATIVE AMERICANS." BUT THAT ISN'T IMPORTANT...
OF COURSE SHE IS. DON'T YOU READ YOUR OWN FILES?
YOUR DATABASE ENCRYPTION ALGORITHMS COULD BE SOLVED BY A MONKEY WITH AN ABACUS, JUST SO YOU KNOW.
I'M USING MY SPIRIT-GIFTS TO TALK THROUGH THE AIR AS YOU DO. SATORI'S KNOWLEDGE OF "ELECTRICITY" HELPED ME DO SO.
SPIRIT-GIFTS? LOOK, WE'RE BEING ATTACKED, AND--
I KNOW. BUT I AM BOUND TO THIS SPOT. I NEED YOU TO BRING THE ENEMY TO ME.
GREAT STRATEGY, THERE, "RUNNING BATHWATER." ARE YOU BEGINNING TO SEE WHY YOUR SIDE LOST YOUR LAND TO A BUNCH OF--
THAT VOICE... I KNOW IT.
MY VOICE?
"...WHAT THAT TRICKSTER, COYOTE, HAS BEEN DOING WITH HIS MICROPROCESSORS." WHY DO I REMEMBER THAT?*
HOW DOES THAT... BEING KNOW YOU? HAVE YOU BEEN PLAYING WITH YOUR PLASTIC INDIANS ON AN OUIJA BOARD OR SOMETHING?
WHEN DID WE COMPLETELY LOSE CONTROL OF THIS SITUATION?
WHOEVER YOU ARE, YOU'RE GONNA GET WHAT YOU WANT. THE ENEMY'S ON ITS WAY.
* PS238 #20

THEN I SHALL PREPARE TO SPLIT THE CLOUDS.
HOLD IT, CRAZY HORSE! KEEP IT IN YOUR BUCKSKINS FOR A MINUTE AND WE MIGHT JUST COME OUT OF THIS WITHOUT WRECKING OUR TEEPEES, OKAY?
I HAVE SOME SENSE OF WHO I WAS, BUT WHY I FIND YOUR VOICE FAMILIAR AND YOUR ARROGANCE UNSUPRISING STILL ELUDES ME.
I GET AROUND A LOT.
NOW KEEP IT DOWN AND LET US RECONFIGURE SOME OF THIS JUNK DOWN HERE...
...BECAUSE IF YOU ARE WHO I THINK YOU ARE, YOU MIGHT BE JUST WHAT WE NEED. STAND BY FOR INSTRUCTIONS!
SO ARE WE BOOSTING THE LETHALITY OF THE SATELLITES AT THE COST OF EFFECTIVE IONIZATION TO IMPRESS YOUR NEW GIRL-FRIEND, OR DO YOU HAVE SOMETHING RESEMBLING A PLAN?
I WANT HER TO IONIZE THE AREA WITH THE HELP OF THE GHOST OF AN INDIAN WHO ALMOST ELECTROCUTED ME ABOUT TWO HUNDRED YEARS AGO, NOT GO WITH ME TO THE HARVEST BALL!
AH, WELL. THAT MAKES SENSE.
SATORI... OR WHOEVER I'M TALKING TO. IT'S VERY IMPORTANT THAT YOU NOT DO ANYTHING UNTIL OUR TEAM IS SAFELY IN THE SCHOOL. DO YOU UNDERSTAND?
IT WILL MAKE THINGS DIFFICULT...
...BUT THEN AGAIN, ATONEMENT ISN'T SUPPOSED TO BE EASY.

MEANWHILE, A CONSIDERABLE DISTANCE AWAY...
HOW ARE YOU DOING BACK THERE, VASHTI?
I AM BARELY ABLE TO FORM THIS SHIELD.
I CANNOT TELEPORT US WITHOUT CONSIDERABLE REST AND MEDITATION, WHICH SEEMS UNLIKELY RIGHT NOW.
WE NEED TO MOVE FASTER!
WHAT I WOULDN'T GIVE FOR EVEN A GO-KART OR--
FRANKLIN!
YOU'RE SUPPOSED TO CALL ME "THE WHIZ" WHEN WE'RE OUTSIDE, AREN'T YOU?
OF COURSE. I'M SORRY, AH, WHIZ.
CAN YOU HELP--
ER, WHAT HAPPENED TO YOUR HAIR, DEAR?
IT'S BEEN SO CRAZY, I HAVEN'T HAD TIME TO GO TO THE NURSE'S OFFICE AND GET IT CUT. MY NAILS ARE GETTING PRETTY LONG, TOO.
THE OTHER SPACE SHIPS ARE GETTING CLOSER...
OKAY, WHIZ...
THIS IS MOON SHADOW.
THE MOON SHADOW?!
YES, DEAR. HE'S... VERY IMPORTANT. WE NEED TO GET HIM TO THE SCHOOL AS FAST AS POSSIBLE.
TAKE HIM TO ANOTHER TEACHER, OR TAKE HIM DOWN TO PS238 YOURSELF, OKAY?
YOU GOT IT!
WAIT, HOW WILL--

PIGGYBACK!
STOP-STOP-STOP-STOP-STOP-STOP-STOP!!!!
-BOOT-BOOT-BOOT-BOOT-BOOT
WHAT'S WRONG?
THAT FELT LIKE I WAS SITTING ON A POGO STICK!
OH. SORRY. MAYBE WE CAN DO SOMETHING ELSE...
OKAY, I GOT AN IDEA! THAT'S HEATHER KLINE'S HOUSE OVER THERE AND SHE'S LEFT THE GARAGE OPEN AGAIN...
WHOOSH!

HEATHER'S PRETTY COOL, SO SHE PROBABLY WON'T MIND US BORROWING HER BIKE LIKE THIS.
'COURSE, SHE DOESN'T KNOW I SIT BY HER IN MATH CLASS EVERY DAY. SECRET IDENTITIES ARE FUN, HUH?
SO WHAT DO THESE SPACE-GUYS WANT WITH YOU, ANYHOW?
DO YOU GOT ANY OF THOSE DARK-MIND POWERS OR ANYTHING HANDY? I HEARD FROM MY FRIENDS THAT YOU CAN DO LOTS OF COOL STUFF.
IS YOUR SCREAMING A SONIC WEAPON OR SOMETHING? I DON'T THINK IT'S HURTING THEM OR--
BZOPT!
FOOMPH!

YAY! I THOUGHT I WAS GONNA MISS OUT ON SAVING PEOPLE!
I CAN PROTECT YOU! THEIR BEAM-THINGS DON'T WORK ON ME IF I'M TOUCHIN' THE GROUND. DOCTOR POSITRON SAYS I'M A NIN-SOO-LATER!
THE ALIENS ARE RIGHT BEHIND US!
CAN YOU MAKE YOURSELF INTO A BALL, WITH US INSIDE?
OKAY! WHAT NOW?
WHOA-WHOA-WHOA-WHA-WA-WA-WA-WA-WA!
I THINK I GOT US AIMED RIGHT AT THE DOOR TO THE SCHOOL!
ONE LOUD "SPLAT" LATER...
WHEEEEEEE... THAT WAS FUN... I THINK.
I THINK... WE MISSED.
YEAH.
HE'S HERE! I'M SENDIN' HIM DOWN PRONTO!
I THINK I'M GONNA THROW UP NOW...

GRAB!
THOOM-THOOM-THOOM
STUFF-STUFF-STUFF
THEY'RE ON THE WAY DOWN. APOLOGIZE FOR ME ABOUT GIVING THEM THE HEAVE-HO INTO THE LOCKER-VATOR.
DOCTOR NEWBY IS STANDING BY.
HERSCHEL?
THE KIDS ARE STILL OUT THERE AROUND THEM STARSHIP THINGS! I CAN'T DO THIS UNTIL THEY MOVE OFF!
SUCH INCONVENIENT MORALITY. IT'S A GOOD THING I PLANNED FOR THIS.
THE SCHOOL'S HOLO-PROJECTORS?
OF COURSE. THIS WILL BE A REHEARSAL FOR WHEN I ADDRESS MY FIRST MILLION-MINION MARCH.
DREAM ON.
SHUT UP. I'M BROADCASTING...

HEAR MY WORDS AND TREMBLE! ALL OF THE LESSER LIFE-FORMS I ATTEND SCHOOL WITH NEED TO VACATE THE AREA. WE'RE ABOUT TO OPEN A MAJOR CAN OF MAD SCIENCE ON THESE TRESPASSERS ON MY PLANET--
"MY PLANET?" DID SOMEONE SLIP SOMETHING IN YOUR JUICE BOX, YOU WHEELBA--
SHUT UP.
SO UNLESS YOU WANT TO KNOW WHAT THE GOOP YOU STICK IN AN E-Z BAKE OVEN FEELS LIKE, GET AS FAR FROM THE SCHOOL AS YOUR PUNY POWERS WILL GET YOU.
IN CLOSING, YOU WILL KNEEL BEFORE VON FOGG. THAT IS ALL.
TRIAL VERSION
PLEASE REGISTER
ENHANCED BY VILLAINCAM.COM
TRIAL VERSION?! BUT I INSTALLED THE CRACK!
OKAY, SATORI... OR WHOEVER... START DOING YOUR THING.

WILL THIS HURT?
NO. BUT I'VE NEVER USED MY GIFTS QUITE LIKE THIS BEFORE...
OKAY...
I HOPE YOUR FRIENDS KNOW WHAT THEY ARE DOING...
CRANSTON? THEY'RE STARTIN' TO DIG.
HOW MUCH LONGER?
SHE HASN'T QUITE GOT HER E.M. FIELD WIDE ENOUGH. WE WANT TO FRY ALL OF THE FLEXI-STRAWS, RIGHT?
GO ON, YOU TWO. MRS. OBERON WILL BE WAITING FOR YOU IN THE GYM WITH THE OTHER CHILDREN.
WE'LL PROTECT THEM! YOU CAN COUNT ON US!
ER... GOOD. THANK YOU,
HERSCHEL, HOW CLOSE ARE THOSE THINGS GOING TO--?
MISTER CRANSTON! IMAGINE MY SURPRISE TO SEE OUR MEETING SHOW UP AS "CANCELED" ON YOUR ONLINE SCHEDULE.

MISS RYLEY, THE ALIENS ARE HERE. NOW!
UNLESS YOU'RE PLANNING TO PICK UP A WEAPON AND GO HUNT THEM DOWN YOURSELF, I THINK YOU CAN MAKE TIME FOR THINGS THAT COULD PREVENT THE CLOSURE OF YOUR SCHOOL!
SO I GUESS EVERYONE WILL FIND OUT I'M MOON SHADOW, HUH?
NOT FROM ME, SWEETIE. WE HAVE DOCTOR-PATIENT CONFIDENTIALITY.
NOW WHEN WE GET THAT NASTY OL' BUG OUT OF YOUR SYSTEM, YOU'RE GOING TO HAVE TO TELL ME HOW YOU WOUND UP OUT THERE TRYING TO SAVE THE WORLD AND EVERYTHING.
I REALLY DIDN'T MEAN TO, I THINK...
WHY ARE THE LIGHTS FLICKERING?
HERSCHEL?
SHE'S BLASTIN' 'EM TO BITS!
YOU HEAR THAT, ZODON? SHE'S BLASTING THEM TO BITS.
YES, VICTOR, BECAUSE OUR CAR WASH MODIFICATIONS TO THEIR SOAP DISPENSER WEATHER SATELLITES DIDN'T INCREASE POWER OUTPUT BY--
MY STAR STUDENTS WANNA LET'CHA KNOW SHE HAD HELP.
THANK YOU.

I REMEMBER... SOME OF WHO I WAS. I STARTED WARS AMONG MY PEOPLE... AND WITH OTHERS...
BUT WHY IS MY CURSE NOT BROKEN? I HAD TO PERFORM A SELFLESS ACT TO SAVE THE LIFE OF ANOTHER.
SURELY I SAVED THE LIVES OF MANY...
PEOPLE..?
ARE YOU SATORI'S "BLUE LADY?"
YOU STILL HAVE WORK HERE, CLOUD-SPLITTER, AND SO DO I.
SATORI, YOU SHOULD RUN AWAY. RUN NOW!
KTHOOOOM!
WE MISSED ONE?!
IT WAS PROBABLY IN ORBIT, WAITING.
I HATE IT WHEN MY ENEMIES HAVE CONTINGENCY PLANS.

I HAVE A SOLUTION, BUT... I WAS SAVING IT TO USE ON HIM.
DON'T FRET TOO MUCH. IT PROBABLY WOULD HAVE FAILED, ANYWAY.
YOU WANNA START GLOATIN' ABOUT IT SO I CAN HEAR WHAT IT IS?
I'LL NEED SOME ASSURANCES FIRST...
DON'T YOU WORRY, SWEETHEART. STASIS IS JUST LIKE GOING TO SLEEP. THAT SPECIAL SUIT YOU'RE WEARING WILL LET US MAKE SURE YOU'RE NICE AND COMFY.
WE MIGHT EVEN BE ABLE TO TALK WITH YOU WHILE YOU'RE IN THERE, BUT THAT'S FOR LATER, OKAY?
OKAY... IF YOU SAY SO.
...FLAGRANT VIOLATIONS OF THE CHARTER, EVEN WHEN YOU STRETCH--
PRINCIPAL CRANSTON? IT'S KINDA URGENT...
IF IT WASN'T, I'D WONDER WHERE I WAS WORKING.
I'M SENDIN' A CONTRACT FOR YOU TO SIGN OVER YOUR TEXT SCREEN. YOU NEED TO CLICK THE "X" AT THE END TO ACCEPT IT, OR WE CAN'T USE THE ONE THING LEFT THAT COULD STOP ALL THIS.
OKAY, LET'S SEE HERE... WAIVER OF TREATY VIOLATIONS... SPACE-BASED MUNITIONS... GAMMA RAY DI-POSITRONIUM CANNON?
THIS ALLOWS ZODON TO GET AWAY WITH USING THE MOON AS A WEAPONS PLATFORM!
I THINK HE DID SOMETHIN' TO AN OLD LUNAR LANDER PLATFORM DURIN' OUR FIELD TRIP.* THE POINT IS, IT'S ALL WE GOT TO STOP THE LAST BATCH OF SPACEMEN FROM DRILLIN' INTO THE SCHOOL.
AND THE LONGER YOU WAIT THE MORE DAMAGE THE DISCHARGE WILL DO TO US!
*PS238 #4

I KNOW I'LL PROBABLY REGRET THIS, BUT...
...AUTHORIZED.
FIRING.
YES.
IT WAS BUILT AND POWERED BY NANITE SOLAR COLLECTORS, WASN'T IT?
HOW PRIMITIVE.
IT WOULD'VE BLOWN A HOLE THE SIZE OF YOUR OVER-INFLATED EGO IN THAT ZEPPLIN-CASTLE YOUR FAMILY LIVES IN.
WOULD NOT!
WOULD TO!
NUH-UH!
YUH-HUH!
WANNA BET?
YOU'LL LOSE.
WILL NOT.
WILL TOO.
NOT TO BREAK THIS UP OR ANYTHIN', BOYS, BUT LET'S AT LEAST GET UNDER A TABLE BEFORE THAT BEAM HIT--
SH-H-KK-DOOM!

HELLO?
IS THIS STASIS?
AM I ASLEEP?
HELLO?
ANYBODY?
CLASS DISMISSED!
PS238

"There is a tragic flaw in our precious Constitution, and I don't know what can be done to fix it. This is it: Only nut cases want to be president."

- Kurt Vonnegut

AARON WILLIAMS'
PS238
TM
27
$2.99
THE WHITE HOUSE
WASHINGTON
SEAL OF THE PRESIDENT OF THE UNITED STATES

PS238
THE SCHOOL FOR METAPRODIGY CHILDREN
BY AARON WILLIAMS
AT LEAST ZODON'S GAMMA-WHATEVER LASER WORKED.
ARE YOU SURE OF THAT?
IF THE BLAST CAVED IN EVEN PART OF PS238, I THINK IT'S SAFE TO SAY THERE'S NOT ENOUGH LEFT OF THE ALIEN SPACECRAFT TO FILL A BOTTLE CAP.
HOW'S YOUR PATIENT?
THE POD'S BATTERIES ARE POWERED. TYLER'S OUT LIKE A LIGHT, AND THE SEALS ARE INTACT.
DID WE GET HIM CONTAINED IN TIME?
ANY CHANCE OF RE-CHECKING?
THE SCANS I DID BEFORE THE WORLD COLLAPSED SHOWED NO ALIEN VIRUSES ON THE LOOSE.
THE SCANNER IS UNDER THE ROCKS TO YOUR LEFT.
SWELL. HOW'S MISS RYLEY?
I'LL HAVE A LOOK.
NOT TOO BANGED UP, BUT... SHE'S UNCONSCIOUS... AND DREAMING?
DREAMING?
HER EYES ARE MOVING LIKE SHE'S IN REM SLEEP. I'M NOT SENSING ANY INTERNAL INJURIES I CAN HEAL...
COULD SHE BE HAVING SOME KIND OF SEIZURE?
I'D CALL UP HER RECORDS BUT MY COMPUTER HAS ROCKS IN ITS HARD DRIVE.

HOW ABOUT YOU? I'M MAKING HOUSE CALLS TODAY.
I'M NOT SURE. A METAL BEAM CAME DOWN REALLY CLOSE TO MY FACE, AND...
WHY DIDN'T YOU SAY SOME-THING? LET ME SEE.
HOW MUCH DO YOU KNOW ABOUT MY "MEDICAL CONDITION," DOCTOR NEWBY?
MEANWHILE, TYLER IS STILL "IN THE DARK"...
CAN ANYONE HEAR ME? HELLO?
I THOUGHT I WAS SUPPOSED TO BE ASLEEP!
IS THIS A DREAM?
IF IT IS A DREAM...
THEN IT'S THE MOST BORING ONE EV--
--THOUGHT I WAS DOING THE RIGHT THING. I NEVER SOUGHT OUT POWER BECAUSE I WANTED IT FOR ME. I THOUGHT I COULD... DO GOOD.
WE ONLY HAVE YOUR WORD FOR THA--

I ALWAYS THOUGHT THAT HEADBAND WAS TO HELP WITH A NEUROLOGICAL DISORDER LIKE PARKINSON'S DISEASE.
THEN I HEARD YOUR JOKES DURING OUR FIRST ORIENTATION AND THOUGHT IT WAS TO HOLD YOUR BRAINS IN.
THAT'S A LITTLE CLOSER TO THE--
THAT WAS CLOSE. YOU STILL THERE?
YESS...
ARE YOU HURT?
NO... JUST... STRAINING.
I'M... HOLDING THE ROCKS... UP.
YOU'RE... TELEKINETIC?
AMONG OTHER THINGS. BUT... IT'S NOT ENOUGH... TO HOLD THE CAVE-IN... FOR LONG. I NEED THE HEADBAND... REMOVED.
WAIT, IT'S... AN INHIBITOR?
YES.
BUT THAT MEANS... YOU'VE ALWAYS HAD MENTAL POWERS?
CAN I CONFESS ABOUT THEM... AFTER WE GET OUT OF THIS?
I VOTED FOR YOU, YOU KNOW.
THANKS.
I'M REGRETTING IT NOW.
I GET A LOT... OF THAT.
YOU DESERVE IT.
I KNOW.

THIS IS HELD ON WITH A DERMAL GRAFTING SOMETHING-OR-OTHER. I THINK I'VE GOT A DEVICE THAT'LL LOOSEN IT.
SOMETHING... OR OTHER?
LISTEN, I CAN PRONOUNCE EVERY PHYLUM OF BACTERIA EVER DISCOVERED, BUT SOME OF THESE WORDS COMPANIES MAKE UP FOR THEIR PRODUCTS WEREN'T DESIGNED FOR MY MOUTH.
AH.
I CAN HEAL THE DAMAGE AS I GO ALONG, BUT I'M NOT GOING TO LIE TO YOU:
THIS WILL HURT A LOT.
DON'T STOP UNLESS THE ROCKS... BEGIN TO SHIFT.
HERE WE GO, THEN...
I SAID, "HOW DID IT GO, THEN?"
MISTER PRESIDENT?
WHAT? OH, SORRY. I'VE GOT A SMALL HEADACHE. IT HAPPENS WHENEVER I TALK TO THE PRESS.
THE ADDRESS WENT WELL, THANKS.

WELL, I'VE GOT AN EVEN BIGGER ONE FOR YOU: YOUR FAVORITE SENIOR SENATOR IS GIVING A SPEECH TONIGHT. IT'S NOTHING BIG, IT'LL PROBABLY ONLY BE ON C-SPAN AFTER MIDNIGHT, BUT...
BUT?
HE'S GOING TO ACCUSE YOU OF EMPLOYING A METAHUMAN TO HELP YOUR POLITICAL CAREER.
OH? AM I HIRING OUT THE POWER PARTNERS TO GO BOOST THE ECONOMY FOR ME?
HIS SPECIFIC CHARGE IS...
...THAT YOU'RE USING A TELEPATH TO INVADE THE MINDS OF OTHER ELECTED OFFICIALS.
WHAT SHOULD OUR RESPONSE BE?
I CAN HONESTLY SAY RIGHT NOW, BEFORE YOU AND ANY DEITY YOU CARE TO NAME, THAT I HAVE NO TELEPATHS, PSYCHICS, MEDIUMS, OR ASTRAL PROJECTORS ON MY PAYROLL. YOU CAN ISSUE THAT AS A PRESS RELEASE.
ALREADY DRAFTED, SIR. BUT...
I'VE BEEN WITH YOUR CAMPAIGN SINCE THE BEGINNING, SIR. AND IT WASN'T MY FIRST. I STILL DON'T KNOW HOW YOU RUN CIRCLES AROUND EVERYONE.
...AND FRANKLY, I THINK I'M BETTER OFF CHALKING IT UP TO NATURAL TALENT.
I'VE ALWAYS SAID IT'S A GIFT.
AND I'VE NEVER BEEN ABLE TO RUN CIRCLES AROUND MRS. CRANSTON.
WHATEVER IT IS... JUST BE CAREFUL. YOU MIGHT WANT TO LOSE A FEW BATTLES, JUST TO THROW THEM OFF BALANCE.
I'LL TAKE IT UNDER ADVISEMENT, MARY. THANKS!

I ALMOST SAID "NATURAL TALENT." I'VE GOT TO BE MORE CAUTIOUS IF EVEN MARY IS STARTING TO HAVE DOUBTS ABOUT ME...
WHAT'S GOING ON?! WHERE AM I?!
I DON'T THINK THIS "STASIS" THING IS WORKING LIKE THEY SAID--
SEAL OF THE PRESIDENT OF THE UNITED STATES
THE WHITE HOUSE
WASHINGTON
Alfred Cranston, President of the United States
Bill,
I looked over your anti-trust proposal, but you must understand my position; what operating system the White
PRINCIPAL CRANSTON WAS PRESIDENT?
OW!

WHY... DID YOU STOP?
I THOUGHT YOUR LUNGS COULD USE A REST. SCREAMING USES UP OXYGEN.
IS THE... AIR... GETTING BAD?
NOT YET. THE DOOR OUT OF HERE IS CRACKED, BUT I CAN'T TELL IF THE HALL IS CAVED IN OR NOT. AND THERE COULD BE FUMES LEAKING FROM THE REACTOR CORE FOR ALL WE KNOW, OR--
I GET THE IDEA. I THINK... I'M A LITTLE STRONGER. BUT THE ROCKS WILL STILL FALL... IF WE DON'T...
BACK TO WORK, I KNOW.
HOW'S MISS RYLEY?
STILL OUT OF COMMISSION. AND STILL DREAMING, I THINK.
SAYS THE TELEKINETIC EX-PRESIDENT. READY?
ODD.
NOT REALLY.
BRACE YOURSELF...

...AND THAT'S THE SITUATION IN THE FORMER YUGOSLAVIA. I DON'T THINK IT REQUIRES IMMEDIATE ATTENTION, BUT THE CONSENSUS IS THAT A MENTION IN YOUR NEXT PRESS CONFERENCE MIGHT SEND THE RIGHT SIGNALS.
I HOPE THIS IS OVER SOON. I CAN'T STAND THIS PAPER-PUSHING STUFF.
THANK YOU, GENERAL WARNER.
JEEZE, WHEN WILL THAT FOSSIL RETIRE?
THE LAST ITEM ON THE AGENDA IS WHAT TO DO ABOUT A BREAKING RUMOR THAT YOUR WIFE COPIED HER MASTERS THESIS TO EARN HER DOCTORATE.
SHE WENT TO WORTHMORE UNIVERSITY? HUH. SMALL WORLD.
SOME WEBLOG IS CLAIMING--
I THINK WE CAN PUT THAT ONE TO REST, MISTER STEPHENS.
SIR?
WE HAVEN'T EVEN INVESTIGATED IT YET, YOU OVER-CONFIDENT--
IT'S THE USUAL SMEAR TACTICS. I READ ABOUT IT THIS MORNING, MYSELF. THEY GOT THE NAME OF HER COLLEGE WRONG.
SENATOR MATHESON SAID THIS WAS ROCK-SOLID. I WONDER IF HE'S GOING SENILE.
OH. THAT'S A RELIEF, THEN, SIR.
I'LL BET SENATOR MATHESON TOLD YOU ABOUT THIS, RIGHT? THANK HIM FOR THE HEADS UP, BUT HE REALLY NEEDS TO STOP BELIEVING EVERYTHING HE SEES ONLINE.
MORE RUMORS, I GUESS.
DID I TURN IN THOSE VOUCHERS? I ALWAYS FORGET...
WHAT'S THAT GUY'S NAME? IF I CAN'T REMEMBER, JUDY WILL BE SO ANGRY...
AND IF THAT'S EVERYTHING, I'LL CALL THIS BRIEFING ADJOURNED!
UGH, THESE SHOES ARE KILLING ME.
THESE MEETINGS ARE A COMPLETE WASTE OF MY LIFE...

OKAY, UH...
"STASIS," I GUESS.
I'D LIKE TO STAY HERE FROM NOW ON. I DON'T WANT ANY MORE MEETINGS OR--
THIS IS A MOST UNUSUAL MEETING, MISTER ALLARD.
CALL ME KENT, IF YOU PLEASE, MISTER PRESIDENT.
AND I THINK ONE OF MY LARGER CAMPAIGN DONORS CAN CALL ME ALFRED.
LET ME BE CLEAR: I DON'T WANT ANYTHING IN RETURN FOR HELPING ELECT YOU. I DONATED JUST IN CASE I NEEDED TO CHAT WITH THE PRESIDENT.
I DON'T THINK THE ETHICS COMMITTEE WOULD FAULT ME FOR LETTING YOU BUY FIVE MINUTES. WHAT'S ON YOUR MIND, KENT?
I INTERCEPTED A FRANTIC PHONE CALL FROM A JUNIOR FBI EMPLOYEE THIS MORNING. HE SAID HE OVERHEARD HIS DIRECTOR HELPING TO PLAN YOU BEING REMOVED FROM OFFICE BY FORCE.
OTHER SOURCES REVEALED THE CONSPIRACY HAS MANY MEMBERS, ALL OF THEM WASHINGTON POWERBROKERS.
TO MAKE A LONG STORY SHORT, I'M HERE TO LET YOU KNOW THAT YOUR COVER AS A METAHUMAN HAS BEEN BLOWN.
AND IF YOU'RE TRYING TO READ MY MIND RIGHT NOW, IT WON'T WORK. YOU'RE NOT THE FIRST TELEPATH I'VE FACED, AND I'VE GOT A FEW MENTAL TRICKS THAT KEEP MOST PSYCHICS OUT.
YOU'RE PRETTY GOOD AT IT. WHAT'S THAT MUSIC YOU'RE THINKING OF?
"SIRIUS" BY THE ALAN PARSONS PROJECT. YOU SHOULD GIVE THEM A LISTEN.

SO YOU'RE NOT HERE TO BLACK-MAIL ME?
I'M MOSTLY HERE TO GIVE YOU A HEADS UP SO YOU DON'T DO ANYTHING RASH.
TO BE HONEST, THAT'S ONLY MY SECOND REASON FOR COMING.
WHAT WAS YOUR FIRST?
TO DECIDE WHETHER YOU WERE A GOOD MAN, A MISGUIDED MAN, OR A POWER-MAD ULTRA-VILLAIN BENT ON WORLD DOMINATION.
VERY DRAMATIC. EVER THOUGHT OF WRITING SPEECHES?
I CAN'T TAKE CREDIT FOR THAT ONE. I BORROWED IT FROM SOMETHG THE BRASS TSAR WAS YELLING AT ME WHEN I TOSSED HIM OFF THE MANHATTAN BRIDGE.
I SEE. WELL, NOW WHAT?
YOU HAVE AN ATTEMPTED COUP TO PREPARE FOR, MISTER CRANSTON. I ESTIMATE YOU HAVE ABOUT A HALF AN HOUR UNTIL YOU AREN'T PRESIDENT ANYMORE.
THIS OFFICE WILL GET VERY CROWDED.
I'D CALL DOWN TO THE KITCHEN FOR SOME SANDWICHES AND REFRESHMENTS IF I WERE YOU.
I DON'T SUPPOSE YOU'D LIKE TO STICK AROUND?
THE PLOTTERS HAVE A BACKUP PLAN THAT INVOLVES A MAN WHO CAN FREEZE YOU SOLID AT A DISTANCE. I'LL BE HANDLING HIM WHILE THE NICE FOLKS OUR YOUNG FRIEND AT THE FBI CALLED TAKE CHARGE OF THINGS HERE.
WHAT DO I DO WHEN THEY ARRIVE?
GIVE THEM THIS.
WHAT IS IT?
A MESSAGE FROM ME. DON'T OPEN IT. THEY'LL KNOW IF YOU DO.
THEY KNOW YOU?
LET'S JUST SAY THEY KNOW THE VERSION OF ME THAT GAVE YOU THE ENVELOPE. AS FOR "KENT ALLARD," HE'S GOING TO VANISH FOR A WHILE.
I'M GOING TO MISS HIM; HE'S ONE OF MY FAVORITE IDENTITES.

OH.
I DON'T SUPPOSE YOU COULD BREAK THE NEWS...
...TO MY WIFE FOR ME?
I WONDER IF MARY KNOWS A GOOD MARRIAGE COUNSELOR?
OR A LAWYER?
I HOPE PRINCIPAL CRANSTON DIDN'T GET US IN TOO MUCH TROUBLE--
OW!
WHY DO DREAM HEADACHES FEEL SO REAL?!

I'M GETTING SOME GRAVEL DRIZZLE, HERE...
S-S-SORRY! HURTS...
I TOLD YOU IT WOULD. HOW'S THE CEILING?
IT'S CRUMBLING... I... NEED MORE. HOW MUCH LONGER?
WE'RE OVER HALFWAY THERE. HOW MUCH ROCK WOULD COME DOWN ON US IF WE DON'T GET RESCUED BEFORE YOUR BRAIN GIVES OUT?
DUNNO. COULD BE JUST... THE ONES IN THAT END OF THE ROOM... COULD BE... ALL OF THEM?
YOU KNOW THIS INHIBITOR WILL PROBABLY GIVE YOU SOME KIND OF NASTY JOLT WHEN IT FINALLY COMES OFF, RIGHT?
IF IT HADN'T BEEN DAMAGED BY THE CAVE-IN... I'D BE A DROOLING... BASKET CASE BY NOW...
TERRIFIC. CAN I CONTINUE?
GO... AHEAD...
GO AHEAD, IT'S OPEN.

SENATOR MATHESON. I THINK WE NEED TO--
PRESIDENT CRANSTON, FOR THE GOOD OF OUR COUNTRY AND THE SAKE OF OUR CONSTITUTION, WE ARE HERE TO REMOVE YOU FROM OFFICE, BY FORCE IF NECESSARY.
ANY USE OF METAHUMAN POWERS OR ABILITIES WILL BE HALTED WITH EXTREME PREJUDICE! UH... SIR.
ARE YOU SURE ABOUT THIS?
JUST KEEP HIM COVERED.
THERE'S NO NEED FOR THAT. I TOLD THEM YOU'D LISTEN TO REASON.
ALFRED CRANSTON
BUT I GUESS THEY THINK OTHERWISE...
ALFRED CRANSTON
IT'S SOME KIND OF MIND TRICK! SHOOT! SHOOT!
BUT HE'S THE PRESI--
HE COULD BE FRYING OUR BRAINS RIGHT NOW! OPEN FIRE!

AW, COME ON! I SAT THROUGH THE BORING STUFF!
I KNOW HE DOESN'T GET SHOT OR HE WOULDN'T BE A PRINCIPAL NOW!
UNLESS...
...THEY MADE A ROBOT THAT LOOKS LIKE HIM...
OKAY, WE'VE GOT A PROBLEM.
JUST... NOW?
FUNNY MAN. THEY'VE DONE SOMETHING HERE I'VE NEVER RUN INTO BEFORE.
YOU'VE WORKED... ON INHIBITOR... DEVICES?
IT COMES WITH THE TERRITORY. ALL DOCS ARE FAMILIAR WITH NEURAL INHIBITORS, JUST IN CASE ONE OF OUR PATIENTS GETS DELIRIOUS.
BESIDES, IF YOU TAKE SOME BRAIN FUNCTIONS ON A LITTLE VACATION, IT USUALLY STOPS WHATEVER ELSE A META CAN DO THAT MIGHT DESTROY THE AMBULANCE.
WHAT DID THEY... DO... TO MINE?
THEY PRETTY MUCH TURNED YOUR HEAD INTO A GRENADE. IF I JUST PULL THIS LAST PART OFF, THE GIZMO DUMPS WHAT POWER IT'S GOT STORED STRAIGHT INTO YOUR CRANIUM.
ANY OTHER... GOOD NEWS?
SURE. IT COULD FRY JUST THE PART OF YOUR BRAIN THAT'S TELEPATHIC. OR THE PART YOU THINK WITH. OR BOTH.
YOU HAVE... TO TRY...

I FIGURED YOU'D SAY THAT. SO I GOT THIS HANDY-DANDY MINI-MRI THAT HERSCHEL INVENTED. HE TOLD ME TO NEVER TAKE OFF THE SHIELDING, SINCE THE MAGNETIC FIELD COULD CAUSE OTHER ELECTRONICS TO HAVE FITS.
LUCKY FOR US, I'M NO GOOD WHEN IT COMES TO DIRECTIONS; JUST ASK MY DADDY SOMEDAY.
I... HOPE I GET... THE CHANCE...
NO YOU DON'T. HE VOTED FOR YOU, TOO.
OH... GREAT.
I'M GOING TO SWITCH ON THE MAGNET AND HOPE IT LETS ME FINISH UNHOOKING THE LAST OF THE HEADBAND WITHOUT ANY FIREWORKS.
IS YOUR OTHER TOOL... STILL GOING TO WORK?
IT'S SHIELDED AGAINST MAGNETIC SUPERPOWERS, SO IT SHOULD BE FINE.
HERE GOES EVERYTHING. TRY TO STAY CALM...
TRY TO STAY CALM, MISTER PRESIDENT. SPELL SYRIN'S MADE US INVISIBLE NOW, AND MANTIUM'S GOT A FORCE FIELD UP.
IT'S SOME KIND OF MIND TRICK! SHOOT! SHOOT!
BUT HE'S THE PRESI--
HE COULD BE FRYING OUR BRAINS RIGHT NOW! OPEN FIRE!
THANK YOU ALL FOR HELPING ME.
THIS LETTER AND YOUR CONFESSION WENT A LONG WAY IN CONVINCING US TO DO SO.

I'D HATE IT IF A BULLET BOUNCED OFF THE FIELD AND SMASHED UP GEORGE WASHINGTON'S HAT RACK OR SOMETHIN'.
THEN I WILL MAKE THEM SEE THEIR GUNS DIFFERENTLY...
HOLY--!
GAH!
YOU GUYS DONE BEIN' COWBOYS NOW? 'CAUSE I THINK TARGET PRACTICE IN THE WHITE HOUSE AIN'T A WELL-LIKED HOBBY.
YOU HAVE NO AUTHORITY HERE! WE'RE TRYING TO SAVE THIS NATION FROM A... A... MIND THIEF WHO USED HIS UNDISCLOSED METAHUMAN ADVANTAGES TO STEAL THE LEADERSHIP OF THE MOST POWERFUL NATION ON EARTH!
PLEASE HEAR US OUT. WE'VE TALKED WITH PRESIDENT CRANSTON, AND HE--
WE HAVE ROCK-SOLID PROOF THAT ALFRED CRANSTON CAN READ MINDS! WE'VE HAD THREE CONCLUSIVE TESTS SHOWING HE'S A TELEPHONIC... SOMETHING....
A TELEPATH, SIR.
A TELEPATH! YES!

WHAT SORT OF TESTS?
REMEMBER THAT RUMOR ABOUT YOUR WIFE THAT YOU CLAIMED TO HAVE READ ABOUT ON THE INTERNET, CRANSTON? THE ONE ABOUT HER CRIBBING HER MASTER'S THESIS?
IT NEVER HAPPENED. THE ONLY PLACE THAT IDEA EXISTED WAS ON MY STAFFER'S AGENDA SHEET. AND THE ONLY WAY YOU COULD HAVE KNOWN ABOUT IT WAS IF YOU TOOK THE THOUGHT RIGHT OUT OF HIS HEAD!
AND IF YOU SAW ANYTHING ABOUT MY FIANCEE, I'LL--
SHUT UP, YOU TWIT.
YOU CAN REST ASSURED THAT PRESIDENT CRANSTON IS PREPARED TO ATONE FOR HIS DECEPTION.
IT'S TRUE. I... CAN READ THOUGHTS.
AND I'VE USED THIS ABILITY TO DEFEAT MY POLITICAL OPPONENTS... WIN ELECTIONS...
GET GOOD DEALS ON CARS...
SEE? SEE?! HE ADMITS HIS CRIMES!
I'M NOT A LAWYER, BUT I THINK THE GUY WHO LED SOME PEOPLE WITH PISTOLS INTO THE OVAL OFFICE SHOULDN'T BE POINTING THE FINGER, EITHER.

MISTER MATHESON, YOU AND PRESIDENT CRANSTON WILL HELP US DECIDE AN OUTCOME TO THIS THAT DOESN'T THROW THE COUNTRY INTO CHAOS.
WE HAVE A LONG NIGHT AHEAD OF US.
AND, YOU, THE ONE WHO WAS CALLED "TWIT." PLEASE GO AND FIND YOUR CO-CONSPIRATORS WHO SNUCK AWAY. REMIND THEM I HAVE RECORDED THE EVENTS THAT TRANSPIRED HERE AND MY TESTIMONY IS ADMISSIBLE IN A COURT OF LAW.
LETS GO BRING THE COUCHES BACK IN. THEY'LL NEED 'EM.
I DON'T THINK WE'VE EVER FINISHED UP WITH TALKING BEFORE. USUALLY WE JUST HIT SOMETHING.
AND WHEN THIS IS ALL SETTLED, I WILL BIND THE AGREEMENT. ANYONE WHO BREAKS IT WILL HAVE.. CONSEQUENCES.
I THINK... I THINK I MAY HAVE IT. IT LOOKS LIKE I'VE REDUCED THE DANGER A BIT, BUT I DON'T WANT--
--EY'RE IN HERE! THIS WAY!
EEEYAAH!
HAARRRGGHH!

--A SCHOOL FOR SUPER-KIDS? YOU THINK THAT WILL STOP THIS FROM HAPPENING AGAIN?
FOR A WALKING SUPER COMPUTER, POSITRON, YOU DON'T SEEM TERRIBLY BRIGHT.
LONG-LASTING SOLUTIONS ARE RARELY SIMPLE, AND REGISTRATION OF METAHUMANS WOULD MOST LIKELY JUST LEAD TO CHAOS AND--
--THOUGHT I WAS DOING THE RIGHT THING. I NEVER SOUGHT OUT POWER BECAUSE I WANTED IT FOR ME. I THOUGHT I COULD... DO GOOD.
WE ONLY HAVE YOUR WORD FOR THA--
--THINK WE COULD RUN A SCHOOL? I USED TO BE A TEACHER, AND BELIEVE ME, IT'S NOT AS EASY AS IT SOUNDS, EVEN FOR THE UNION OF JUSTICE!
THIS WAY, THE CONSPIRATORS RESIGN, WE KEEP THEIR SECRET, AND WE MIGHT PREVENT THIS CATASTROPHE FROM REPEA--
--THE INSTALLATION OF THIS INHIBITOR OF YOUR OWN FREE WILL?
YES, YES. I SIGNED THE FORMS, SPELL SYRIN WILL SAY HER HOCUS-POCUS OVER IT, SO JUST GET ON WITH--
ME? PRINCIPAL? BUT WHY?
WELL, IF WE GOTTA SWITCH JOBS, WE MIGHT AS WELL BRING THE GUY WHO'S RESPONSIBLE, RIGHT?
'SIDES, YOU KINDA COME RECOMMENDED, THANKS TO THAT ENVELOPE YOU GAVE US WHEN WE SAVED YOU.
YOU'D PROBABLY BE SAFER WITH US, TOO.
SO WHAT WAS IN THAT ENVELOPE, ANYWAY?
JUST A CARD.
R
I think he means well.
WHOEVER GAVE IT TO YOU WAS PROBABLY SOMEONE IN DISGUISE, SO DON'T BOTHER--

THEY MADE PS238... BECAUSE OF SOMETHING BAD PRINCIPAL CRANSTON DID?
AND WAS THAT KENT GUY... THE REVENANT?
AND... THE UNION... OF JUSTICE... ARE OUR TEACHERS... THAT'S... AND...
ZZZZZZZZZZZ...
I SAID I WAS SORRY IF MY ASTRAL FORM FRIGHTENED YOU, DOCTOR NEWBY. I WAS LEADING YOUNG ZACHARY AS HE TUNNELED HERE.
YOU NEVER TOLD US YOU WERE A METAHUMAN YOURSELF.
FUNNY HOW THAT WORKS.
BUT I'M NOT THE ONE WHOSE BRAIN YOU MAY HAVE DAMAGED. I HEALED HIM AS BEST AS I COULD, BUT I'M NOT GIVING CRANSTON A CLEAN BILL OF HEALTH UNTIL I CAN EXAMINE HIM SOMEWHERE WITH A SECURE ROOF.
AND GOOD NEWS, THE TOTAL COUNT FOR EXTRATERRESTRIAL VIRUSES IN THE AIR READS ZERO. LUCKY FOR US WE GOT THE CEILIN' BRACED BEFORE IT COLLAPSED.
SPEAKING OF WHICH...

HOW LONG DOES THE MOLECULAR CEMENT YOU SPRAYED ON THESE ROCKS NEED TO SET UP? THE LONGER I HAVE TO BE A SUPPORT STRUT IS ONE MORE YEAR THE WORLD WILL EVENTUALLY SUFFER!
WHAT'S THIS... WHAT'S HIS NAME? TYLER? WHY IS HE IN THIS STASIS MODULE?
OBVIOUSLY, HE'S INFECTED WITH THAT VIRUS THE ALIENS BROUGHT.
I THOUGHT IT WAS THAT "MOON SHADOW" CHARACTER WHO HAD IT?
IT COULD HAVE MUTATED AND BEEN PASSED TO NORMAL-BOY, THERE.
AND IF IT DID, DOESN'T THAT MEAN IT'S STILL ACTIVE, BEING SPREAD TO THE WORLD?
I DOUBT IT. THAT LOOKS A LOT LIKE HIS CAPE OVER THERE.
AH, GOOD. PROBLEM SOLVED, SO LONG AS NOBODY DIGS HIM UP.
YOU MEAN... MOON SHADOW IS... GONE?
I THINK WE NEED TO GET TO THE SURFACE AS SOON AS WE CAN, ZACH. CAN YOU LEAD US OUT AND MAKE THE TUNNEL BIG ENOUGH FOR TYLER'S POD?
I... I THINK SO... BUT MOON SHADOW... WAS MY HERO...
OH, FOR MOTHBALLS SAKE...
EVERYONE HEAD 'EM OUT!
ZODON, THAT WALL WAS SET ABOUT FIVE MINUTES AGO. WHY'RE YOU STILL IMITATIN' A CAR JACK?
YES, OF COURSE, MOCK THE PERSON WHO SAVED THE PLANET...

LATER, OUTSIDE OF EXCELSIOR SCHOOL...
I GUESS IT'S A GOOD THING THE SHIP WAS HALFWAY TO PS238 BEFORE IT DETONATED.
OH, YEAH. ZODON'S BEAM BLASTED THEM BACK EIGHT GENERATIONS. MY GUYS FROM CLAY INDUSTRIES SHOULD HAVE EXCELSIOR RIGHT AS RAIN INSIDE OF A WEEK.
PS238 WILL TAKE A BIT LONGER, BUT...
DO YOU THINK WE CAN REBUILD HERE? AFTER THIS?
IT'S NOT LIKE THE INVASION WAS A SECRET. IT WAS WORLDWIDE.
TRUE.
AND THE KIDS ARE TELLIN' THEIR FOLKS THAT THEY WERE FOLLOWIN' MOON SHADOW'S LEAD WHEN THEY TOOK ON THE ALIENS.
THAT SHOULD CUT DOWN ON LAWSUITS.
AND THAT LADY AT K-SQUARE STARTED A CANDY BAR DRIVE TO HELP PAY FOR RECONSTRUCTION.
I ALREADY ORDERED YOU A CASE OF THE ONES WITH CARAMEL.
THANKS. ANY CASUALTIES?
WE DON'T THINK SO. SOME PEOPLE AIN'T ACCOUNTED FOR YET, BUT IT'S NOT LIKE OUR EQUIPMENT'S UP AND RUNNIN' TO MAKE A QUICK TALLY.
EVERYONE WE KNOW THAT WAS IN RANGE COULD HANDLE THE BLAST... BUT, AH... MISS KYLE WOULD LIKE TO SEE YOU.
IS SOMETHING WRONG?
WELL, REMEMBER HOW OUR ORIGINAL PLAN HAD JUST ONE SPACESHIP, AN' SHE WAS GONNA PUT THIS THING ON IT THAT WOULD ATTRACT LIGHTNIN' FROM THE WEATHER SATELLITE?
YES...
SHE STILL HAD IT ON HER WHEN WE ZAPPED 'EM ALL...
OH...
YES, "OH."
MISTER CRANSTON. IN THE RECENT PAST, I'VE HAD MY POWERS TURNED UP SO HIGH I COULDN'T MOVE, I'VE BEEN INTERROGATED BY AGENTS OF THE FEDERAL GOVERNMENT, MY CAR WAS JUST VAPORIZED IN THE PARKING LOT, AND ON TOP OF IT ALL, I JUST GOT MY HAIR HIGHLIGHTED AND PERMED LAST WEEK.
OH.
THERE'S THAT "OH" AGAIN...

...AND IT WAS JUST HIS CAPE, STICKING OUT FROM UNDER ALL THOSE ROCKS! AND THEY SAID HE HAD A VIRUS OR SOMETHING, TOO!
BUT HE'S MOON SHADOW! HE CAN'T BE... WELL, DEAD. CAN HE?
I THOUGHT HE WAS SUPPOSED TO BE ABLE TO TURN INTO A CLOUD OF BAD DREAMS OR SOMETHING. THAT'S WHAT SUZI TOLD ME, ANYWAY.
I NEVER SAW HIM DO THAT.
BUT MISTER CRANSTON SHOULD KNOW, HE WAS DOWN THERE. LET'S GO ASK HIM.
THEN WE'RE DONE? I CAN LEAVE TOMORROW?
I THINK THE SCHOOL CAN MAKE DO WITHOUT YOU.
THANK YOU. I'VE BEEN PLANNING TO GET AWAY FROM THIS PLACE FOR MONTHS NOW.
MISS KYLE IS QUITTING OUR SCHOOL?!
THIS IS HORRIBLE!
DOES THIS MEAN I'M NOT GETTING A "C" IN HER CLASS ANYMORE?
CLASS DISMISSED!
PS238

PS238 SKETCH GALLERY

OTHER BOOKS BY AARON WILLIAMS:

- Ps238, Volume I:
  With Liberty and Recess for All
- Ps238, Volume II:
  To the Cafeteria, For Justice
- Ps238, Volume III:
  No Child Left Behind
- Ps238 Volume IV:
  Not Another Learning Experience

- Full Frontal Nerdity:
  Epic Fail

- The Nodwick Chronicles Volumes I & II:
  Haulin' Assets
- The Nodwick Chronicles Volume III:
  Songs in the Key of Aiiieee!
- The Nodwick Chronicles Volume IV:
  Obligatory Dragon on the Cover
- The Nodwick Chronicles Volume V:
  Tour of Doodie
- Nodwick: *Adventure Log*

ACKNOWLEDGEMENTS

Thank you to everyone who keeps kicking me in the butt and pleading that no matter what I do, that I should never stop creating more ps238. My beloved wife, Cristi, does this on an almost daily basis, and I don't think I would have come this far without all of the encouragement.

Thanks also to Wildstorm editor, Scott Peterson, for his kind words to me as I, like so many others, dumped bound paper into his lap, hoping that it might lead to fame and glory. I also thank him for his even kinder words after, words that let me know I was doing a whole lot of things right.

Thanks to my family, who understands as best they can why summer isn't a time for vacations, that conventions are as much about doing a job as having fun, and that holidays sometimes mean I have to stare at a laptop while everyone else is watching the game on TV.

But thank you, most of all, to you, the reader. For all your feedback, your patience, your help, and your support. These books couldn't exist without you, and I hope that you treasure them as much as I do.

Now if you'll excuse me, I have to find out what happens next so I can pass it along.

ABOUT THE AUTHOR

Aaron Williams is a cartoonist, writer, and blogger living in Kansas City, Missouri with his wife and darling of every convention they attend, Cristi. His art credentials include work for the former print publications Dragon Magazine, Dungeon Magazine, the City of Heroes comic book, and having a degree in Political Science.

His current projects include the webcomics "Full Frontal Nerdity" and "Backward Compatible," both of which cover interests both geeky and nerdish. He also tends to run off at the keyboard a lot at his websites, Nodwick.com and ps238.com. He also throws out links to strange and arcane parts of the web, for which his readers forgive his ramblings.

Ps238 is currently his only regularly printed production, although his work has appeared in other venues. He's written scripts for Marvel and DC comics, and hopes to do bigger and better things with a few major comic companies in the near future.

Aaron attends far too many conventions for his own good, designs t-shirts of dubious cultural value, and tries to play enough video games so that he can understand what people under the age of fifteen are talking about. Someday he hopes to "pwn" someone, but he freely admits that sometimes just having a goal is enough.